The C

Evasion in Lockdown

The Cleaner

Evasion in Lockdown

Rachel K Parsonage

First published in 2021

Edited by Alison Williams

Cover design by Davenports Printers

ISBN 978-1-914406-04-1

The Cleaner: Evasion in Lockdown

Kyle Joseph is in the final year of his GCSEs. He lives on an estate where drugs and gangs are rife. Impressionable, he makes a bad decision, and finds himself embroiled in a county lines drug-dealing gang. With no way out, Kyle takes the only action possible to save his own life and the lives of others who are being exploited by the gang.

For a few months, it seems that the problem has gone away. Kyle gets on with life, gets his head down in school and starts a new job as a cleaner in the local hospital. Then lockdown hits. Desperate to recruit members, the drug-dealing gang is back. As hard as he tries to distance himself, Kyle soon finds that declining the offers of work from the gang is not an option. Trapped, can Kyle evade the gang in the middle of a pandemic?

Dedication

To my lovely auntie, Mrs Susan Youngman, a born fighter and survivor.

To my darling nephew Ruben. RIP, little man, miss you forever.

Chapters

2nd April 2020

Kyle arrived in intensive care. Another body bag was being moved from the 'COVID positive' area. Intensive care staff scrubbed and washed the specialist equipment that Kyle and the other cleaners had been told not to touch. Kyle was glad that he didn't have to go anywhere near it; what if he pressed a button by mistake? Or broke one of the tubes? What if he ended up killing someone? A nauseous feeling rose in his chest at the thought. Michelle, his supervisor, appeared beside him. She was puffing like a steam train after racing up the stairs to respond to the emergency bleep.

'Kyle, we're going to have to get a move on in here, they're just moving this body to the morgue. Another patient is due in, just been flown in by helicopter, they're waiting in A&E resus, needs a ventilator apparently.'

'OK, Michelle'.

'There are no other spare ITU beds in the whole of North Wales, nearest one is now Liverpool.'

Kyle's heart began to beat faster. What had happened to the part-time cleaning job that he had applied for in the morning before school? Mopping the hospital floors? Cleaning ward surfaces and around patients' beds? Scrubbing the toilets? How had he ended up here, partly responsible for ensuring the safe passage to intensive care of a patient with a life-threatening illness?

'None at all?'

Michelle shook her head.

'How long have we got?'

'Less than fifteen minutes if we can,' said Michelle, rolling her eyes. 'That's why I've had to come up, you'll never do it by yourself.'

There were no short cuts in intensive care, nothing that could be left for next time, and no way of missing anything out. Everything needed to be done thoroughly. Kyle made his way into the changing room, pulled his suit on and collected his cleaning supplies. He could feel the vibrations of the room through his hazmat. The patients in this part of intensive care were all COVID positive, anaesthetised and relying on ventilators for every breath. They didn't look like people, they didn't move, or talk. They just lay there, wrapped in all kinds of tubes and equipment.

Sweat dripped down Kyle's face as the suit steamed up. He looked up at Michelle who pointed to the entrance. Like a colleague in a nuclear power plant, or an actor in a movie scene reminiscent of a scene from an apocalyptic disaster, she was indicating that they had to leave. But this was not a nuclear power plant, or an apocalyptic disaster, this was a British National Health Service hospital in 2020.

As Kyle finished mopping the floor, a team of medics appeared at the door with a patient lying on a trolley enshrouded in resuscitation equipment. The plastic at the front of Kyle's mask had long since clouded over and his armpits were sopping.

Kyle began to undo his the hazmat suit as he made his way out of ITU and into the changing rooms. He discarded it in the clinical waste bin together with the rest of his protective equipment. What a relief. He looked up at the clock – it was nearly time to go home: he couldn't wait to get into the changing rooms and have a shower.

'Well done, mate,' said Michelle, following closely behind him with her hair plastered to her head and beads of sweat dripping off her nose. 'We did it.'

'Yeah, just about.'

When he had started this job, he had known exactly what it was that he needed to do. He had a schedule, a routine. There were no such things as face masks, or hazmat suits. Because of his age, he could only work for limited number of hours, no nights, no anti-social shifts. Whether this was an antisocial shift was questionable, but with the hospital short of cleaners, nobody had batted an eyelid when he had applied to work for a few hours before school every day. Now, in the space of just under two months, things had changed. They were changing every day, every hour, sometimes every minute. Kyle didn't like it.

Outside in the fresh air, Kyle breathed a sigh of relief as he left the stale, clinical environment. He felt human again after his shower. As he made his way home, his thoughts turned to what he'd just seen at work. He'd not seen the face of the patient in the body bag and he was glad. Regardless, he wondered who it was; had they been unwell anyway? Were they old? Had they known they were going to die? In the hospital, because of COVID? Did their families know?

As he walked home deep in thought, Kyle realised that he had reached Jade's old house. It was still cordoned off by red tape and metal fencing that had long been kicked in; burned out, looking as forlorn as ever. COVID had stalled any plans that anyone had of renovation. Always a reason to make him smile. As much as he realised how badly it could have all ended, Kyle grinned to himself. It had been nearly six months since he had last seen Daryl. He wondered if the police had caught up with him yet? Was he still on the run? Kyle felt certain that he wasn't; he would have come looking for him by now, wouldn't he?

One thing was for sure, the hospital was the last place that Daryl would come looking for him, wasn't it? That said, cleaning the COVID-filled wards of the local hospital could never, ever be worse than working for Daryl. Had Daryl executed his plans, Kyle could have been one of the occupants of the body bags making their final journeys through the corridors of the hospital – if anyone had ever found him that was. He shuddered to himself as he contemplated the possibility.

Eventually, he reached the park. Covered in litter from the increased lockdown footfall, it was more of a mess than usual. Kyle usually avoided walking through the park when he was on his own, but today he didn't care. He was tired and wanted to get home as soon as he could. As he crossed the car park by the shops, he heard a voice.

'Alright, Kyle?'

Kyle stopped. His blood froze. Slowly, he turned around. Daryl.

1st July 2019

Kyle inhaled deeply and blew out the cigarette smoke. It was a glorious day. The summer sunshine beamed down on the school field as he and the other smokers congregated underneath the shade of the big fir tree. He took another drag of the cigarette and handed it back to Mo. Mo took it, then paused.

'Aw, man! Quick, everyone, hide your fags, Marchant's over there,' he said as he stubbed the cigarette out and placed the remainder on the stone wall behind them. 'By the old stile on the road.' Everyone hastily disposed of their cigarettes.

Lunch breaks when Mr. Marchant was on duty consisted of him finding novel and innovative methods of catching pupils smoking. Today - attempting to be as evasive as possible - he had crept behind the old stone wall that separated the school grounds from the road. Climbing over what was formerly a stile in years gone by, he precariously balanced on the top. Eventually, he took the plunge and jumped into the clump of well-established blackberry bushes on the other side. He screeched in pain as his thin spindly leg became trapped. Eventually he freed himself from the tangled undergrowth. Kyle, Mo and everybody else looked on, sniggering, as he cursed and shook his leg. Seeing them standing there with no cigarettes, minding their own business, seemed to infuriate Mr. Marchant even more.

However, standing behind one of the fir trees, oblivious, Barry continued to puff away on the cigarette that he had obtained from Ishmael. Ishmael didn't smoke but he was being "encouraged" to purchase a regular supply of cigarettes for Barry. Eventually, Barry registered the fact that Mr. Marchant was advancing at significant speed towards him.

'Quick, hold me fag!' he said to Ishmael.

'No, I can't, Barry… they'll kick me out this time.'

'Just hold it, before I leather you!'

Ishmael fearfully took hold of the cigarette. Barry tried, but failed, to creep inconspicuously behind the nearby fir tree.

Ishmael was one of the many kids in school who lived in care. He had only been attending since February. He had told Kyle all about his past. He painted a bleak and dismal picture of life before he was removed from his family home. Ishmael's eyes emitted a dreadful sense of melancholy which seemed to follow him around everywhere that he went. There was an air of desperation about him, a pathetic sense of wanting to belong somewhere, anywhere, even if it was to the worst club in the world. Unfortunately, this rendered him vulnerable. Ever since he had come to the school, he had been trying to fit in somewhere, to be accepted. Sadly for Ishmael, the school bully, Barry – who by now had managed to alienate himself from the majority of his peers - had taken full advantage: Ishmael was a perfect commodity for him to use. Kyle liked Ishmael.

'Well, what have we here? Ishmael Ali! And you, Barry Tomlins, come out from behind that tree immediately!'

Barry emerged. A spiral of smoke trailed up Ishmael's back and rose into the air. Mr. Marchant's beady eyes scanned them, eventually fixing on the top of Ishmael's head as he noticed the wispy trail wafting over it.

'Aah!' said Mr. Marchant, pointing his long, bony finger towards Ishmael. 'Now tell me, what do you have behind your back?'

'Wot? Me? N…n…nothing, sir!'

Mr. Marchant crept closer to him. 'Show me your hands!'

Ishmael pulled one hand out from behind his back, then the other. The trail of smoke that had previously crept up from behind his back was now wafting up from the ground at his feet. Mr. Marchant spotted the cigarette burning on the grass. He beckoned to Ishmael.

'Right! You can come with me!'

Ishmael looked up at Barry in despair, waiting for him to say something. Barry remained silent. Mr. Marchant frogmarched Ishmael towards the school.

Tall and well built, Barry threatened anyone who failed to do what he told them to. Ishmael had already been in trouble several times, taking the blame for Barry's actions and was on his final warning before expulsion. Barry was aware of this; evidently he didn't care.

Ishmael wasn't stupid. Over the past few months Kyle had got to know him. Behind the exterior of the frightened little boy who was petrified of being abandoned again was a hopeful spirit who wanted to succeed and learn. He pretended not to be interested in school but he went to his lessons and he achieved reasonable grades. Barry was grinning to himself. The grin dropped away from his face as he caught Kyle's look of contempt.

'Well, fess up, Barry, otherwise that's Ishmael out.'

'What? Dopey git! Fancy dropping it on the floor and not putting it out first!'

Kyle picked his cigarette up from where Mo had strategically placed it behind the stones and re-ignited it, continuing his stare off with Barry. Barry shrugged and picked up the burning cigarette that Ishmael had dropped.

'Yeah, but Barry, then you'd have had a go at him for squashing your fag. Fancy letting him take the rap for you, man!'

Barry's face fell. 'What?' he said as his face scrunched up, like a bulldog chewing a wasp. 'And get into shit meself? Na!'

Barry had done some evil things to people in the past, but this really was too far. His cowardice was evident, his contempt for Ishmael brazen. Barry seemed confident that Ishmael mattered as little to Kyle as he did to anyone else.

Kyle watched as Ishmael was escorted down the field by Mr. Marchant; as he listened, he could hear him pleading with the teacher not to phone the foster home where he lived.

'Aww, come on, Barry, aren't you meant to be hard?' Kyle asked, blowing smoke in Barry's direction. 'Why you letting him take the rap? It was your fag, if you're so hard, what you letting him get into shit for? He's taken enough for you as it is!'

The gang fell silent, all eyes on Kyle and Barry. Barry shifted around uncomfortably.

Kyle had had many arguments with Barry over the years, and, funnily enough, despite all the intimidating threats that Barry had made to "kick his head in" etc., the threats had never materialised. Things had come to a head earlier in the year when Kyle had called him out over calling his best friend Mo a terrorist because he and his family were Muslim. Barry had threatened to "deck him". Kyle had advised him to proceed, but Barry had declined to do so, stating that he would "kill him". Despite Kyle's further invitations, he then had stormed off into school claiming that the teachers were coming and that he would finish him off later. He never had.

'Ahh, what does he matter anyway? Who is he? Yer new boyfriend?'

Kyle held his arms out widely to the sides.

'Well, it's just that I thought you were meant to be hard, Barry. Or are you just hard when it's someone you think you can start on and they ain't gonna say anything?'

'Fair warning, Kyle, shut your gob if you don't want a hiding.'

'Whatever, go and tell Marchant the truth if ya meant to be so hard, Barry! That's Ishmael's final warning here.'

'Yeah, well, I'll… I'll… I'll flatten you.'

Kyle let out a snigger as he handed the cigarette back to Mo.

'Barry, the only thing you could ever flatten is your own turd if you sat on it!'

The group collapsed, guffawing as they tried to muffle their sniggers. Barry's face turned purple.

'Yeah, but it's true though, innit?' said Kyle as he turned to face the rest of the group.

'Right, you've… you've had it now!' said Barry as he swung his huge arm towards Kyle. 'Time for a decking; get back home to Africa where you came from.'

Rage bubbled up in Kyle. He ducked out of the way of Barry's arm. Barry's centre of gravity shifted as he stumbled forwards. Before Kyle could stop himself, his right arm had automatically pulled itself backwards: it flew forwards, straight into Barry's nose. Barry sank to the floor in a heap as blood poured out of his nostrils. He lay on the floor, not moving. Everyone gasped.

'Mate, I think you've killed him!' said Mo.

Kyle bent down and poked his finger into Barry's face, squelching the bottom jowl of his large flabby jaw. Barry moaned.

'Na… he's still alive.'

The bell rang.

'Catch ya in a bit, Mo!'

Kyle hurried back down the field towards the school, leaving the group standing with their mouths open. Mr. Marchant was heading across the netball court with Ishmael in tow.

'Sir,' said Kyle to Mr. Marchant as he drew level with him, 'the fag you accused Ishmael of having, that was Barry's - Ishmael doesn't even smoke, Barry just makes him buy them for him.'

Luckily, Barry had regained consciousness by the time that the ambulance arrived. Barry's status as the hardest kid in the school was destroyed as a new school legend was formed: Kyle Adams, the guy who knocked Barry out cold. However, due to the fact that he had been suspended for a month, Kyle wasn't there to revel in any of it.

His mum was furious. She grounded him for two weeks and stopped his pocket money for a month. She made him do all the work that they sent home for him. Even though Kyle found it easier to study when he sat on his own without the distractions of school, it got so boring after a week or so.

'Can't I just leave this bit? I hate history anyway, Mum?'

'Very funny, you'd better start getting your head down in that school. I don't scrub toilets all day so that you can chuck your life away.'

'Yeah, yeah, Mum!'

Kyle's mum worked as a cleaner in the local hospital. She got up early to go to work and was back home by the time Kyle got home from school. She wasn't like everyone else's mum; she always knew where he was. She went to every parents' evening, phoned the school on a weekly basis to make sure that he had turned up and even had a rota on the wall of when his GCSE coursework was due.

30th August 2019

The final rays of the summer sun glared through Kyle's bedroom window. The window was huge, which would have been great if the view hadn't been of the uninspiring concrete blocks of post war housing, now a sad testimony to the failed ideology upon which it was based. It was grim.

Kyle was bored. So much so that he had even wished that school would re-start. After a few weeks, the summer holidays had lost their charm. There were only so many times that he could go to the park and play football with his mates, so many games that he could play on his computer, and only so many things he could buy with the sparse amount of money that he had before it ran out. His mum was at work until mid-afternoon. That meant that he had to make his own dinner every day. Furthermore, to his dismay, their usual summer holiday to Devon to see his aunt, uncle and cousins had been cancelled due to the fact that his uncle had been unwell.

But this morning, Kyle had woken up early. He was excited! He looked at his phone, it was seven a.m. Not long now! Unlike most mornings, when Kyle got out of bed at the latest possible moment, he got up immediately and jumped into the shower.

He loved to spend time at his grandad's house down the road. They usually went to watch their beloved Wrexham play, but football had finished for the summer. Recently, Grandad had spent a lot of time away from home helping his friend Cliff. When Kyle was little, his gran and grandad had had a stall on a Victorian market at an old harbour by the sea. Grandad's friend Cliff was the harbourmaster and on the harbour was an old ship and a lighthouse. Kyle used to spend his weekends there with his grandparents. Grandad was going up for a couple of days and this time, Kyle was going too. They didn't go back there often now as Grandad had had to relinquish his driving licence and consequently his stall. This made it even more special because today, they were going on the train. Just as Kyle finished his breakfast, there was a knock at the door.

'Come on then, mate,' said his grandad. 'We'd better get going.'

'Nearly ready, Grandad.'

Kyle loved spending time with his grandad. He felt comfortable talking to him about things that he didn't like talking to his mum about; he didn't have to pretend, or lie, or try to be cool. He could just be Kyle. Grandad was ace. He had emigrated to Britain with his family in the 1950s and had lived here ever since. He had married Kyle's nana, a fellow immigrant who was from Trinidad, and they had eventually settled in the small town in North Wales. Kyle loved hearing Grandad's stories. The ones about how people had been racist to him made him feel sad. But Grandad usually managed to find humour in them somewhere. He had thick skin. While his mum had been furious at Kyle for being expelled from school for knocking Barry out, Grandad, even though he had scolded Kyle for missing his work, had just laughed.

They made their way into town to the train station where they caught the train up to the coast. Kyle looked out of the window as the train stopped and started again at the towns and villages along the way, with the houses and the fields flying past, filled with toy-sized animals grazing.

His heart beat faster with anticipation as he waited for the train to reach the point where he could see the big ship on the coast - and there she was. Kyle's heart leapt with joy when he saw her, the only vessel for miles around, as if she had just been dropped there like a giant invader from out of space, looming out of the sea, forlorn. She was docked just before the muddy banks of the estuary where the inland disappeared to make way for the sandy beaches of North Wales, the estuary funnelling to the point where it spilled into the Irish Sea. And he knew that he was getting near to the harbour and the lighthouse. There it was! Cliff had had the lighthouse brightly painted in red and white rings. She stood out of the sea on guard. Kyle could hardly contain his excitement.

The train stopped at the once grand but now shabby Victorian station. They made their way to the centre of the vibrant seaside town. It was the last week of the summer holidays and the place buzzed with holidaymakers. Children trailed around after their parents, gorging on ice-creams, and carrying an array of plastic toys that would make them happy for an hour or two, purchased from one of the many shops displaying their wares outside - shops that all sold the same thing.

They dodged the crowds and stopped at 'spoons' for a fry up. The place was heaving with the usual holidaymakers who had popped in for breakfast and the regulars who frequented the pub from morning until closing time, sipping away on their 11 o'clock pints on this glorious sunny morning.

'What shall we do, Grandad? Do you want to walk up there or get the bus?'

'To be honest, son, I'm a bit stiff from sitting on the train, shall we walk it?'

Kyle nodded enthusiastically. He loved the costal path walk from the town to the harbour where Grandad used to keep his stall. It was just under a mile long. Once they had finished their breakfast, they left the humdrum of the town centre and headed back towards the path by the sea. As they proceeded along the path and turned the corner of the bay, Kyle gulped in the fresh sea air. Although it smelled slightly salty, it tasted of nothing; no petrol, no diesel fumes, no cigarette smoke, no staleness. It was if he, Kyle, was the first person who had ever inhaled it. As they turned the corner of the bay – there she was, the big ship, standing right in front of them. Behind her was the lighthouse.

From this part of the shore, unless you took another twenty minute walk around the bay, the lighthouse and harbour was only accessible to the public by boat. In the sea next to the site was an ancient row of large stones next to a rock inlet which stretched from the beach to the lighthouse and the harbour on the other side where the abandoned ship lay. The stones were relics of the path placed there hundreds of years ago to reach the lighthouse. Kyle had walked over them many times when he was younger and knew where to step without even looking. They were large and relatively safe as long as the sea was calm. At low tide, the surfaces were uncovered. But as the tide rose, they became largely invisible to the untrained eye. Anyone who knew the path could still cross it, although the choppier the sea became, the more perilous the path across. Across the fifty metres or so of sea, Grandad could see Cliff on the side of the harbour painting the stern of a boat. He whistled across to him.

'Oi, Cliff.'

'Stay there, I'll send the boat across,' yelled Cliff.

'No need,' said Kyle's grandad.

'Are we taking the stones, Grandad?'

'Aye, for old time's sake?'

The tide was coming in. Grandad leapt over the partly submerged rocks with the agility of an eighteen-year-old. Kyle followed close behind. After forty metres or so, they reached the lighthouse. Then there was the easy part - the next ten metres to the harbour where Cliff was working.

'Ahoy there…' said Grandad.

'Len! Come on over, I'll make you both a brew, although I should have sent the boat, you shouldn't be jumping over those rocks at your age,' Cliff said with a laugh.

'Sod off, you'll be my age in a couple of years,' replied Grandad.

A short while later, Kyle and Grandad sat with Cliff on the harbour, drinking tea and reminiscing over old times. Kyle observed people as they walked up and down the costal path. As he stared out to sea, Kyle could see the landmarks of Liverpool and the Wirral. He watched the traffic in the distance; a passenger ferry, a cargo ship and an oil-tanker. Business like. Buzzing around the busy sea in what seemed like a faraway world from the calm of the North Wales coast.

'You been up to much, mate?' asked Cliff.

Kyle shook his head. 'Na, just on summer holidays.'

'So what's this? Your last year of school?'

Kyle nodded.

'What then?'

'Dunno. Suppose I'll have to get a job.'

'You don't sound convinced, Kyle.'

'Well, I don't do very well in school.'

'Why, mate?'

'I don't know, I just don't see the point.'

Grandad put his tea down.

'Look, I keep telling you, take it for what it is and just go, get your head down and do the work.'

'But it's so boring, Grandad.'

'But once you've done your exams, you'll never ever have to go again, but you've got something to say to your potential employer, '"Look, I didn't fart about in school, I'm a responsible person".'

'I just can't get my head down in there, Grandad. I get distracted. I wouldn't even go if my mates weren't there.'

'A lot of those kids that you're hanging around with, in a couple of years, they probably won't even feature in your life, except for a few like Mo. You'll probably never see them again.'

'Anyway, do you want to take your stuff to the lighthouse and freshen up?' asked Cliff, in a subtle attempt to distract them from the increasingly heated discussion. 'Just put it in the big cupboard at the bottom with the key.'

Kyle nodded enthusiastically.

'I'll set us up some camp beds after the last tour,' Cliff said. 'Doris is happy because she doesn't have to cook me any tea tonight.'

'Right, son, go and get changed, then get the lid off this paint and let's get painting some of these metal railings for Cliff,' said Grandad, as he finished his tea. 'He's getting too old and decrepit to be doing it all by himself.'

'Shut up, you fossil.'

Kyle grabbed their bags. He gazed up at the lighthouse which towered above him. The late summer sun bounced off the bright white and red rings painted on the façade. Despite the fact that it was daylight and the light at the top had long since become obsolete, it was as if the outside of the lighthouse shone regardless. The thick, ancient wooden door was open. Kyle stepped inside and looked around at the old concrete stairs, curving around the inside all the way to the room at the top. He placed the bags in the cupboard and leapt up them, looking out of the windows as he went. From here, he could see right across the estuary to Liverpool and the Wirral with all the landmarks intact. He looked down to the deck of the old ship below, forlorn with paint peeling off. Kyle loved it here. At the top of the stairs, the light-filled room at the top boasted even more generous views of the surrounding areas as the sun's rays bounced off the whitewashed walls of the interior.

At the top was an old room containing the huge light. It had an old desk and chairs. It was where Grandad and Kyle would be staying. Although Len had invited them to stay in his house which was adjacent to the site, realising that he would have to climb the stairs, Grandad had declined, knowing that Kyle loved staying in the lighthouse.

Once back outside, Kyle and Grandad set about helping Cliff. Watching the fresh cream paint cover the old black of the harbour railings was therapeutic. It gave Kyle time to think, not about anything in particular, just to think. By late afternoon it was time to stop. They had painted a substantial amount. Cliff had finished his last tour of the day.

'Shall we leave it there, kid?' asked Grandad. 'It's six o'clock.'

Time had flown. Kyle had thought that it was still much earlier than that.

They got an Indian takeaway with Tiger beer for tea and sat in the cabin of Cliff's boat on the harbour, eating and drinking. The weather had become slightly chilly for a late August evening, and a cold North West wind blew in to the coast. Kyle gulped his beer contentedly as he watched the calm sea. This was a good time, this was better than any holiday.

The next day, Kyle and Grandad finished painting the metal railings. Then they took one of the little boats out into the sea and went fishing. Kyle caught some mackerel to take home for his mum. After, Cliff took them to a nearby pub for Sunday lunch and they wandered back to the lighthouse. Then they had a cup of tea outside, watching the sun go down. Kyle felt like a millionaire as he took pictures on his phone so that he would not forget this glorious moment! Cliff had asked him not to upload any pictures to social media in case they drew unwanted attention to the site so Kyle saved them on his phone. He would look at them from time to time - he would know that he had been there.

Before he knew it, Kyle's holiday was over. He was gutted. He could have stayed for longer, much longer. But it was time to say goodbye to Cliff and the lighthouse. Cliff gave them a lift to the station and they boarded the train back home.

Kyle still had another week before school started. Soon it would be autumn. The football would be starting again soon; he could go to see Wrexham play with grandad. After his trip to the lighthouse, hanging around the streets with his mates and smoking whatever they could get hold of didn't seem as appealing anymore.

11th September 2019

'Kyle, what the bloody hell is this about you skiving off school again?'

Kyle drew in a deep breath in as he tried to finish his maths homework. He knew she'd find out – she always did. How he wished that he had stayed in school yesterday. He had been thrown out of his history class for messing around, so he had come home early as he didn't see the point in hanging around for P.E.

'Well? Answer me, Kyle.'

His mum was not happy with him at the moment. Even though it was only September, he was already in trouble in school for missing a couple of lessons here and there. She had confiscated his phone yesterday after she had accused him of being rude. All he had said was that he had crap trainers compared to the ones that his mates had! She had hit the roof and accused him of being rude, obnoxious (whatever that meant) and having a bad attitude.

'Well, what was the point of me staying at school? I got told off and they said I had to sit in detention; I didn't see the point in staying there just for P.E.'

Kyle braced himself as he heard her storming up the stairs. The bedroom door flew open.

'You're going downhill, Kyle! What do you think you're gonna do when you leave school? Hang round this estate with the other dropouts? Piddle around like you do now?'

'No!'

'Well. What you gonna do?'

'I'll get a job.'

'Where you gonna get a job with no qualifications? Somewhere for minimum wage where you have to toe the line? How you gonna cope there being told what to do if you can't even tolerate being told what to do in school, or by me?'

Kyle shrugged. 'Yeah, well, it's not my fault there's no decent jobs round 'ere.'

Kyle had never had much money. His mum never had much money. He had not yet received his national insurance number. Last year, he had tried to do a paper round, but it had ended up being cancelled because too many people had failed to pay.

His mum huffed. 'Well, get your head down in school, pass some exams and move somewhere where there is one then… you don't have to stay in this hole.'

'What? Where I don't know anyone? Na, I'll stay here, with my mates.'

'Even most of your mates will have moved on by then, well, the ones with any sense will have, maybe not the stupid ones…'

'Stop calling my mates stupid, they're alright!'

'I like to think that most of them are, but if they're skiving off school with you, and doing the same stupid stuff that you're doing, then they must be stupid as well!'

Kyle shrugged. Deep down inside, much as he hated to admit it, he knew that his mum was right, there were no decent jobs round here. A lot of people that he knew didn't work. Those that did had jobs that Kyle didn't really fancy doing and they seemed as poor if not worse off than people who didn't work. She was right, what on earth was he going to do when he left school? What was out there for him? What future?

In school, most of the kids didn't care, it seemed like the teachers didn't care, no one else's parents seemed to care, no one except for his mum. She was always on his case. He had to do his work, every evening after school before he went out unless he went to football. She was even more on his case now as it was the final year of GCSEs.

'Why can't I go out now? Why are you making me do this? I'm not even sitting the exam!'

'I don't care! Don't come down 'til you've done that sheet, and then I want to see it.'

'You're nuts making me do this.'

'What did you dare to say?'

'Nothing, mum.'

Kyle had equations to practise for his maths GCSE. Equations? The only point in maths was to add his money up. *When am I going to use equations, for crying out loud?* When Kyle did his work himself, he found that he could concentrate. But, once he got into school, it was noisy, and people picked on you if you knew the answers. He found learning in the negative, oppressive environment daunting. He figured that there was really no point in even pretending that you were clever or interested and risk being called a swot!

'I mean seriously, Kyle, what do you think…'

His mum continued to yell at him. Kyle's mind drifted off and he stared out of the bedroom window at the glum view. Rows of houses that all looked the same. Occasionally you'd see streets or a house that was a bit different, where things weren't the same, where someone had done something nice to their house. But on this part of the estate, those were the types of houses that got burgled. It was as if everybody else knew that there was no point in making their gardens or the fronts of their houses look nice, or different. Furthermore, the ones that nobody cared about took the shine off them, somehow. Even when the sky was blue, it made no difference. Once the bright rays of the sun hit the earth around there, they were subsumed to mere darkness, eaten up by the surrounding concrete misery. This was further reflected by the demeanour of most of the people who lived there. They walked around with faces that looked uniformly sad and hopeless. An air of despondency prevailed. In the end, it was as if everyone just accepted it and started acting as glumly as their surroundings.

'Are you even listening to me, Kyle?'

'Well, who are you to lecture me about education? What have you done with your life that's so great?'

Kyle's mum's forehead was furrowed, her eyes narrowed. 'What have I done? I spend eight hours a day scrubbing that hospital, to keep a roof over your head! That's what I do.'

'Yeah? Well, did you have to go to school to get your job? No, you didn't, did you? So why do you make me do homework? And keep telling me that I've got to go to school when I don't want to? It's not as if you did it yourself, is it?'

'Kyle, don't you dare speak to me like that! And to throw the fact that I work as hard as I do back in my face? Who do you think you are? What are you going to do that's so great with no GCSE's?'

'Well, you got GCSEs. I'm not being funny, Mum, but you work, and all you do is moan about how crap your job is, and that you've got no money. So why bother? Why not just go on benefits like everyone else round here?'

Her jaw dropped open in disbelief.

'Go on benefits? Are you serious? I'd have less money than I've got now! Is that your answer? To go on benefits?'

'Well, there are loads of other people round here who don't work. They're on benefits, but they buy their kids smart trainers, they don't complain about being skint…'

'Yes, Kyle.' His mum was getting so cross that she was beginning to hiss at him. 'And where do you think they get their money from? Selling drugs, to wreck other people's lives. Or doing something dodgy. Then they get caught, then they end up in jail. A bit like Mohammad's brother and his dad!' She put her finger to her head as if to indicate that Kyle was stupid for not making this connection for himself. 'Now Mohammed, there's a person who isn't stupid. Why can't you be more like him?'

'Yeah? Well, at least his family doesn't have to walk round in crap trainers, and at least people who sell drugs have money.'

'No, Kyle, they walk round in shoes paid for by blood money! Watching their backs to see where the next drug dealer who's waiting to pounce on their patch is going to emerge from, probably with a knife in their pocket, knowing that if they're lucky, they'll not be dead or in jail in a year. How much money do you think his mum's got now his dad and brother are in jail?'

'Yeah? Well, at least they get respect, and a decent car, and…'

His mum angrily poked her finger into his chest.

'Don't you dare tell me about how great it is to be a drug dealer! Are you stupid? Just because you want a new pair of trainers? Are you that thick? It's obvious that even Mo realises this, why can't you?'

'Yeah? Well, why did you bring me up round here then? Why didn't you get a better job and move somewhere else if it's that bad?'

'How dare you? You really are one ungrateful shit! And don't you dare start telling me that it's better to go on benefits, or sell drugs than work hard for a living; jeez, I've failed!'

Kyle couldn't understand why his mum was so mad: it was true! Most people who lived on the estate didn't work, preferring to turn to other means to obtain money. The ones that did worked in monotonous jobs that were nearly as boring as being on the dole. Who could blame those that didn't work? The local drug dealers got more respect than the working folk of the estate. Deep down, he knew that it was wrong, but it was just… normal. It was as if the longer he lived here, the more normal it all became.

How Kyle wished that he could go back to the lighthouse with Grandad… far away from this place!

'You're not even listening to me, are you? Seriously, Kyle, your attitude is a disgrace...'

She went on and on and on.

At the last parents' evening, his mum had been told that, although he was capable, it was doubtful that he would be put in for all of his GCSEs. This was mainly due to his lack of attendance and his bad attitude in school. Not that Kyle cared: what was he going to do with qualifications anyway? His mum, however, had been furious. She still made him do the work regardless, hoping that the teachers would change their minds.

'Anyway, you need to change some of this,' she said, thrusting the English paper that he had given her yesterday in front of his face.

'I took ages doing that! Change what?'

'Don't tut at me, Kyle! It's not bad, there's just a few bits you need to redo.'

He had to hand in the essay for the stupid English exam! One that the teacher said that it was likely that he wouldn't be put in for! He had spent ages writing it. It had taken him three days! Now she was saying that he had to change bits! The deadline wasn't even for a week. English! What did he need to study it for? He could read and write! Wasn't like he was going to be an English teacher or something, was it?

'Yeah, whatever.'

'Kyle, you're going to do this, and you're going to pass your exams. This is the only way you're ever going to get out of here and do anything.'

'What for?'

'Anything, Kyle, get a decent job, go to college, join the circus if you like! But you can't do things while your aspirations finish at the end of this estate.' She gestured towards the window. 'You need to see the bigger picture of life.'

Kyle huffed. 'Yeah, alright.' He sighed reluctantly as he sat back down to work.

'Anyway, I've underlined the bits that need changing; have another look at it, correct it and then hand it in tomorrow. It's done then, isn't it?'

Kyle started making corrections. Even though it was boring, it seemed clearer. If only his teachers were this helpful instead of just chucking him out of class all the time. Eventually he finished his work and printed it out to take to school.

'Can I go out to the skate-park to meet Mo and the others for a game of football?' he asked.

'No, it's getting dark earlier, Kyle, you know how dangerous it can be down there; it's too late to go now.'

'Mum, I'm fifteen, and I'm taller than you. Who do you think's gonna bother with me?'

'It's not who is going to bother with you that I'm worried about, Kyle. It's what you're going to get into down there, the drugs, gangs and all the rest of it.'

Kyle didn't reply. He stopped listening as she reiterated the dangers lurking on the estate; she's said all this so often that it had become clichéd - such issues didn't even sound like threats anymore.

'I've done my work.'

'No, you can't go out, not if you're skiving off school. You're going to stay here with me, and we're going to watch a documentary about drug dealing, and we…'

'Sod that, I ain't stayin' in here, I've done what I said I was gonna do.'

'Oi, you, get back here…'

Kyle stormed out of the house and slammed the door, ignoring his mum's requests to come back.

He knew that she wouldn't be happy when he went home later, but the thought of staying in all evening when he knew that his mates were out playing football at the park was too much to bear. He would just have to take the bollocking when he got back.

The sun lay low in the late September sky with its final bright rays radiating over the land. Even the last glorious rays failed to light up the sprawling concrete mass below. The occasional areas of green on the park that did contain trees and grass were places where no one wanted to go; people took their dogs to do their business there so they didn't have to clean it up, and they injected their fixes out of sight behind the overgrown shrubbery, discarding the remains into the sprawling undergrowth.

"The park" was a sprawling area in the middle of the estate, adjacent to the abandoned train station which had been shut in the 1960s as part of the Dr Beeching cull. Years ago, before the estate was built, the area was upmarket and well kept. All that remained was a sprawling mass of wasteland with no identifiable purpose. "The park" was where the working boys and girls congregated in the old train station at night and where dubious activities occurred. Easily accessible with a car park for the supermarket right outside the entrance, it was the perfect place to engage in illicit activity. Right at the end on the other side there was a smaller park with equipment for younger children and a football pitch. In this park, hypervigilance for items such as needles, dog muck and broken glass was required. Visiting the park with children was not the experience that had originally been intended.

As Kyle walked along, he mulled things over. He was bored and fed up, fed up with feeling like he had no purpose in life. He hadn't meant to upset his mum, but what he had said to her was true - out of all his friends he always seemed to be the one that had the crappier pair of trainers and the more basic phone. He was secretly envious of some of his friends. Even though some of their parents were on the dole, they always seemed to have money to spend, new clothes and a decent phone. Kyle's mum hardly ever had any money. She didn't drive and was always very clear with him that he couldn't have the things that he asked for. Strangely enough, she was quite happy to pay for other things, things that weren't that essential. When he complained that he was struggling with his maths, she got him a tutor. That was thirty pounds an hour! When his football boots got robbed, she went straight out and got him some more. When they went on the school trip to France last year, she paid for it, it was £150! But she refused to buy him the latest pair of Adidas or Nike Air trainers or a new bike when he had one already; she said that she would pay for things that he needed, not things that he wanted. Was she crazy? Didn't she know that he'd get picked on for having crap trainers? Kyle just couldn't understand how little she could care about him! Oddly enough, most of his mates' parents - even the ones that seemed to buy them new trainers and phones - had told them that they couldn't afford the trip to France. Kyle didn't get it!

He had loved the school trip. It had been epic and he remembered every minute of it; travelling on the ferry, the buildings, the language, the landscape. Ever since, he had loved his French lessons and was actually on course to pass his French GCSE. His mum had been pleased with him. If he could do stuff like that, actually see what he was learning and how it was all relevant, Kyle always found it much easier to learn.

Since he had knocked Barry out, Leanne, who was really fit, had taken an interest in him. She usually went out with older boys, ones who had a car and stuff. But she had told Mo that she liked Kyle. Kyle had been round to her house a few times and they had ended up getting off with each other. Rumour had it that she was seeing an older guy who had a car. If only Kyle could get some new gear, and some money together, maybe he could impress Leanne enough for her to be his girlfriend? Then she wouldn't feel the need to see other blokes.

Some of the gang were congregated on the skate ramp - the safest place to sit: hazardous items stuck out like sore thumbs on the smooth concrete.

'Is it clean?' asked Kyle

'Yeah, couldn't find no needles. Anyway they're all over there behind the bins, still there now. They must be wrecked,' replied Mo.

Kyle could just about make out a group of the local drug users congregated behind the concrete shield of the bins.

They ended their game of football as dusk fell on the park. Gradually the others drifted off home. Kyle and Mo sat musing things over and shared a cigarette that Mo had robbed from his older brother.

'Mo, I'm in shit, dude.'

'Why?'

'She found out about me getting chucked out of class, and knew I'd come home after.'

'Oh.'

'She's just had a right go at me. About how I'm never going to get a job if I don't do my work. It's like I told her, she's got a job, and what for? She's never got any money. We live here, she won't buy me any decent trainers!'

'Mate,' said Mo, 'everything you've got in that house, she's paid for it. She cares about you, man. I've got decent trainers, but sometimes I go home and there's hardly any food in the house. And you haven't got people knocking at your door, taking your telly or the fridge, or your mum getting a knife to her throat because your dad owes people money.'

'Seriously?'

Mo nodded. 'Yeah, my mum has never got any money, not when my dad goes back inside. And now our Shashif's gone as well, she's got even less.'

'Shit, man. I had no idea.'

'No, mate, I see homeless people with better trainers than me. It doesn't mean they're having a better time.'

Kyle began to feel ashamed. Ashamed that he had judged and treated his mum like that. Ashamed in front of Mo, someone whose dad and older brother Shashif were in jail for drug-related offences. Mo's mum had to look after him and his brothers and sisters on her own. To Mo, he, Kyle, must seem so ungrateful.

'Sorry, Mo, you must think I'm a complete tosser. I don't mean to sound like a knob.'

'No, man, but all the stuff, the trainers, the cars, the new phones, the bikes, it's all false. It doesn't mean anything. It could all go, at any time. They're just a hair's breadth away from being nailed at any second.'

'Well, you're lucky though, Mo, at least you know who your dad is.'

Mo looked up at Kyle. He was about to say something. But before he could do so Jason entered the skate park on his bike.

Jason was in the year above Kyle and had just left school. Kyle hadn't seen him for a while. He looked different to usual. He was wearing a brand new Nike tracksuit and brand new Adidas trainers, the ones that Kyle had asked his mum to buy him. He pulled out a brand new iPhone; a few kids in school had one. His mum, as usual, had told him to whistle when he had asked her to buy him one.

'Alright, Jase?'

'Yeah, not bad, not bad.'

'Nice gear,' said Mo.

'You working?' asked Kyle.

Jason nodded. 'Sure am, sure am! Yeah, well, this and that, you know. Earning a packet to be fair, delivering parcels for a new firm that's set up.'

'What? Like Amazon?'

Jason shook his head. 'Na, none of that paying tax or minimum wage crap, it's all underground, if you know what I mean. But they have got some vacancies.'

Kyle nodded.

'Either of you interested in earning a bit of cash?'

Mo shook his head. 'Na, mate.'

'Maybe,' said Kyle.

Kyle felt Mo's eyes burning into him. Mo was one of Kyle's more sensible friends and he tried to stay on the straight and narrow. He could smell trouble like other people could smell a rat.

'It's easy, I've got one here. All you got to do is take it to the arranged drop; twenty quid I've been getting'.

Kyle sat up. 'Twenty quid? For one drop? What's the catch?'

Jason shook his head. 'No catch, mate, you take the parcel, you get your money. Happy days.'

Twenty quid? Just for delivering one parcel to someone?

'I'll do it.'

'But Kyle, you said we were going to…'

'Na, Mo, mate, it's OK.'

Jason looked around. There was no one there save for the drug addicts behind the bins. He pulled a package out of his tracksuit top and handed it to Kyle.

'Here, all you got to do is take it to this address, you might know it… it's my sister Jade's.'

Jason gave Kyle the address.

'Yeah, no problem.'

'I've got a few to take, and I won't be able to do them all in time.'

'Right, yeah, cheers, Jase.'

Jason nodded and rode off. 'Catch you later, guys, let me know if you change your mind, Mo.'

'Yeah, cheers, mate,' said Mo unconvincingly.

As soon as Jason was out of earshot, Mo turned to Kyle.

'Kyle, mate, what are you doing?'

'What? Mate, I'm skint, I'm sick of having no money, I'm sick of living in this shit hole with nothing to look forward to. Twenty quid for a delivery to one address? I'm there, man'.

Mo put his hands up in the air.

'Kyle, mate, you know what's in there, don't you?'

Kyle shrugged. 'Na, mate, I'll risk it for twenty quid!'

'Yeah, it's a shit hole, but if you end up getting involved in shit like this,' he pointed to the package, 'you'll end up in far worse shit!'

Kyle shrugged again. 'Mate, what does it matter? It's one drop.'

'Mate, it starts off like that, I've seen it all before! Look, you can always get out of here somehow, but get involved in this, you'll end up in jail, or in some gang, or like the guys behind the bins over there.'

Kyle shrugged again. 'Well, I ain't going to, mate. I know what's in here.'

'Exactly, that ain't gonna be new shoes is it? Or a birthday present off her dearest aunt?'

'Well, no, but twenty quid? Come on…'

'And it's his sister! Of all the people he's dropping to, how's he got time to pop to the park and talk to us but he can't go to his own sister's? He's bullshitting you, man! These people, they've reeled him in, and they'll reel you in!'

'Mate,' said Kyle, 'chill, I know what I'm doing. I'll just do a couple. When I've got a bit of money, I'll finish.'

Mo put his head in his hands.

'It doesn't work like that, bro, once you're in a gang, you don't just leave… why do you think every time my brother comes out of jail, he ends up back in there? Seriously, mate, don't do it!'

Kyle put his hand on Mo's shoulder. 'Look, bro, thanks for your concern, but I'm sick, sick of all this. I'm skint, I've got nothing, I'm never gonna have nothing! Even when I tried to do a paper round, that got cancelled. There's nothing else round here.'

Mo stood, shaking his head. 'It's better than you'll be in a few weeks, trust me, bro.'

'Look, dude, I'll catch you tomorrow. Don't stress, it's cool!'

Kyle walked off down the path, leaving Mo staring after him. Kyle knew what the matter was, Mo was scared. Mo had seen it all, his house being raided, the ducking and diving, the police coming round, the drug dealers waiting to jump them outside the house. But one package? To Jade's house? What harm could it do?

Jason's sister Jade had always been troubled. She had taken drugs for as long as Kyle could remember and had drifted in and out of jail for various minor offences. She was only twenty-two, but looked much older. She had a few missing teeth, was extremely malnourished and haggard from taking the amount of drugs that she did. Her house – frequented by men - was situated on one of the less desirable streets of the estate at the far end near the main road separating the estate from town.

As Kyle walked he ruminated over what Mo had said. Mo was his best mate, and was looking out for him. He spoke from experience and Kyle respected that. But twenty pounds? For one drop? What harm could it do? He could maybe do a few and then stop?

In a way, Kyle envied Mo. Despite his difficulties at home, he had people around him. Mo knew who he was, he had a dad. Kyle had never known his dad. His mum didn't like to talk about him. On the odd occasion that his dad had been mentioned, Kyle's family were remarkably scathing about him. Kyle got the feeling that his dad was someone he would rather not know, or was so bad that no one wanted him to know who he was. But the main reason that Kyle felt odd about not knowing his dad, was because Kyle's dad did not share his mum's heritage. The rest of Kyle's family were black, and it was obvious that his dad was white. Growing up in this town in North Wales which was predominantly white, Kyle found himself walking around, wondering if every guy walking past him was his dad.

There was only him, his mum and his grandad. He had an aunt, uncle and cousins who lived down in Devon. When they were all together, Kyle never felt that it was a problem. But to the outside world, Kyle sometimes felt that he looked like an outsider in his own family. He sometimes wondered about the other side of his family, about what his dad had done that was so bad. When Kyle and his mum argued or he thought that she was being unfair on him, he wondered if she was just being horrible to him because he was a permanent reminder of a mistake that she had once made. They had never discussed the matter and his mum had never passed comment about how different he looked to her. Kyle could never fathom if this was just how it was when you were raised by a single parent, or if it did have something to do with his colour. Whatever it was, it had certainly left him with questions that he would have liked answering. Maybe his sensitivity precluded his inherent hatred of people like Barry being racist to Mo? Mo - the most sound and finest guy that Kyle had ever met.

Kyle aspired to belong somewhere, to be noticed, to be someone, to be cool. But the only people that he knew on the estate that had cars, and money, and respect, were the local drug dealers and gangsters. Kyle knew that he didn't want to be in a gang, or end up taking drugs. He just didn't know what else he wanted to do. Surely if he worked for them for a bit, it would be OK?

Jade's house looked miserable in the fading light. In fact, all the houses in this street were grim. The area was notorious for crime. Despite the waiting list for social housing, houses on this street remained unoccupied and boarded up. The constant hum of traffic from the main road was evident and the air tasted of fumes. The front pane of glass on Jade's door had been smashed and the garden was full of rubbish. Kyle knocked at the door and waited, holding the package. A wiry man, dressed in a leather jacket and retro Adidas trainers, opened it. His green eyes pierced into Kyle's intensely.

'Come in, mate,' he said, in a curt southern accent.

Odd, the man was not who Kyle had been expecting. He looked, well, normal. Well-groomed, he seemed almost polite. Not like the usual people that Jade hung around with. Kyle walked into the house, puzzled. Jade was sitting in the corner, off her face as usual. She smiled up at him. There was another man sitting in the corner, a large, thick-set man with a scar that ran across the bottom of his face for about an inch from both ends of his mouth. He didn't smile back at Kyle.

'The name's Daryl. You are?'

'Kyle, er, I know Jason, he asked me to bring this,' said Kyle, handing over the package.

'Oh, er yeah, of course… thanks. I'm Daryl, a mate of Jason and Jade's; just a little business we've got going on here, making a few quid, dodging the tax man, if you know what I mean.'

'Yeah, that's cool,' said Kyle, nodding.

'Yeah, just a new business for the local community, delivering parcels, quick delivery, no questions asked.' He fished a twenty pound note out of his pocket and handed it to Kyle.

'Er, cheers,' Kyle said.

'No problem, no problem at all. And thank you, thanks for helping us out tonight. And if you're interested, we could always use reliable people, good rewards. Aren't there, Jade?'

'Alright, Jade?' said Kyle. She nodded.

'Aw, excellent, you two know each other then? This is Bert.'

Daryl indicated the tall, thick-set man. 'He runs one of our other operations in another area. There are a few of us up and down the country. We're always looking to expand, take on new staff, go into business with people like Jade here.'

'Yeah, sounds good.'

Another man walked in. He was in his early twenties, good-looking, and wore fashionable, designer clothes. Kyle had seen him around. He drove a customised orange BMW. Kyle always thought that he was so cool when he drove past him in it. He handed Daryl a package.

'Daryl, man, I can't keep coming to the house. You need another bic, mate.' He said.

'No worries, no worries, Nathan, mate, it's all in hand.' Replied Daryl, winking at Nathan.

'OK, see what you mean, pal.'

'Yeah, nice one mate,' said Daryl. 'Great rewards; like Nathan here, can afford his own smart car and clothes.' He handed Nathan a wad of money as he turned and walked back out.

'Plenty more work where that came from; in fact, we've got some going tomorrow evening if ya free?'

Twenty quid? For one delivery? Kyle began to think about all the stuff that he could buy! He could be free tomorrow night. 'Er, yeah.'

'Great, easiest money you'll ever make, mate, ask no questions, cash in your hand at the end of the night. Got a few new recruits round here delivering parcels.'

'Yeah, great.'

'Excellent! Swing by here, at, say, five?'

Kyle contemplated this for a few seconds. What harm could it do? Just a few more parcels and then he could get some trainers, like the ones that he had asked his mum to buy him. He nodded at Daryl.

'See you tomorrow then.'

As Kyle went to leave, there was another knock at the door. An older man walked in.

'Jade, darlin', your client's here,' said Daryl.

The man who had just walked in looked around sixty. He was overweight, bald and unkempt. Jade stood up and led him upstairs.

Kyle left, wondering what the set up was. At first he had wondered if Jade and Daryl were together, but she didn't seem like his type. He seemed streetwise, intense, as if he had plans, and an agenda. And he hadn't flinched when the man had arrived and Jade had taken him upstairs. Jade's only agenda was to get her next fix of heroin. Maybe she'd recruited Daryl as her pimp, to look after her, to help with her business transactions. That must have been what he meant when he said that they'd gone into business together. Jade was usually that off her face that she would undoubtedly find it difficult to manage anything more than her next hit herself.

Regardless, Kyle walked home with a spring in his step. Now he had twenty pounds in his back pocket! He had previously been paid that for delivering two days of papers. This was the easiest money that he had ever earned! He felt rich!

****

'Man, what were you thinking last night?' asked Mo in school the next day

'How do you mean?'

'Doing deliveries? For Jason? Who was it for?'

'Aw, some bloke who's living with Jade.'

'What? She's got a boyfriend?' Mo asked, incredulous.

'Don't worry, it's cool. Just a little business they've got delivering stuff from her house.'

Mo shook his head. 'Mate, I'm telling you, it's dodgy as. Whatever you do, don't go back there.'

'Mate, I earned twenty quid for one drop, just a few more and…'

'Mate, Jade's gone in the head, there's only one reason she'd have a bloke there operating from her house,' said Mo, putting his head in his hands.

'Well, maybe, but I'm gonna do a couple of deliveries, then jack it in when I've got a bit of cash.'

Mo shook his head. 'Mate, you need to watch it...'

'Na, mate, how can it go wrong? I'll do a couple of deliveries, then stop.'

Mo shook his head again. 'Trust me, Kyle, I've seen it all before. People don't just turn up living with someone like Jade, handing out innocent packages, and giving you twenty pounds to deliver each one… before long, you'll get reeled in… working for twenty quid a day if you're lucky and you won't be able to leave.'

'Yeah, but a few days' work, that's all I'm doing, then I'll leave.'

'Dude, you don't just leave gangs like that, and if they've just landed there, at some random off their face person like Jade's house, it sounds like county lines to me.'

Kyle shrugged. 'Na, mate.'

He had heard of county lines drug dealing - that was when they forced kids to sell drugs for gangs up and down the country just by using one mobile phone. He respected Mo's opinion, but there was no way that he, Kyle, could be forced to do something against his will, was there? He could not deny that there was something about it all that felt odd and weird, but twenty quid, for one delivery?

'Na, mate, just a couple.'

'Mate, stop being so stupid! Listen to me! In a few weeks, you'll be a dead man walking!'

Kyle sighed. The gang and the set-up, the bloke with the weird scar, they did seem, well, scary.

'Yeah, OK, then, Mo, I'll stop.'

Mo slapped Kyle hard on the back. 'Thank god you've seen sense.'

19th September 2019

'Goal! Yes!'

Mo had kicked the ball into the net. He jumped up and down with exhilaration, eventually landing on Kyle's back.

'Winners! We've got to be! There's only two minutes to go!'

'Yeah, we haven't won yet…' replied Eddie, ever the pessimist, patting Mo on the back.

The sun was beginning to set over the mountains outside town. Kyle zipped up the jacket of his brand new Adidas tracksuit. There was no doubt that the weather was getting colder. As they finished their football game, no further goals were scored.

'Inside next week, lads,' said Charlie, the coach. 'Then we're gonna have to start charging subs again to hire the room.'

The team nodded. Charlie knew that although his football team was talented, most of them had little in the way of disposable income. He had managed to come to an arrangement with the local sports centre whereby he used the pitch for free and they only paid if they had to hire the room inside or the Astroturf. Kyle's mum always made sure that he had money to go to football.

He had spent the money that he had earned from Daryl on an Adidas tracksuit top. He really wanted the bottoms to go with it, but he just couldn't afford them. He had asked his mum and she had said no. The cheap supermarket bought jogging bottoms that he had on were becoming worn and faded. She had snapped at him when he had asked her why she wouldn't she buy him the rest of the tracksuit.

'There is nothing wrong with the ones that you have. You can wear them until you need some more.'

'But Mum, they're faded, and no-name!'

'I don't care, Kyle. And I really don't believe that you bought that top off one of your mates for a fiver with your pocket money! Not unless it's been robbed.'

Kyle had not replied. His mum was suspicious of him; one thing that she wasn't was stupid. It wasn't unheard of to buy knock off gear in school occasionally, but it was an excuse that he couldn't use too often.

What's more, Leanne had been sitting outside, watching with her mates. Kyle had felt her eyes bearing into him as he played. He felt sure that if he looked a bit better, she'd fancy him even more. Rumour had it that she was getting serious with this other bloke that she had been seeing. He had a car and everything, what chance did he, Kyle have, going round in supermarket sports gear?

Kyle bid Mo goodnight and made his way home. As he left the park, he could just about make out a figure circling the car park on a bike. It was Jason.

'Orait Jase?'

'Yo, Kyle. Not seen you around. Thought you might want to deliver a few more packages for us?'

Kyle ran his hand through his hair. 'Yeah, no, I'm good, thanks, mate.'

'Come on, I've got another one here, another twenty quid? It won't take long.'

Kyle remembered the promise that he had made to Mo.

'No, man.'

'Look you'd be doing me a favour. I haven't got time to get them all done tonight. It's easy money, the easiest money you'll ever earn.'

'No, dude, I'm good.'

Jason sighed.

'Well, if you're sure. New top, man? Looks cool.'

'Yeah…' said Kyle, hesitating. It did look cool. Kyle knew that he could look even cooler if he bought the rest of the tracksuit. At the moment, there was no way that he was getting it this side of Christmas.

'Go on,' said Jason again, handing Kyle a package. 'Twenty quid.'

Twenty quid – what harm could it do? Who would know? Reluctantly, Kyle took the package.

'Yeah, OK.' Kyle tried to justify it in his mind. Just another package. Maybe he could deliver one now and again?

'Nice one, mate. You won't regret it.'

'Yeah, cool man.' Kyle looked at the address; Jade's house again. He shrugged.

Kyle needed to hurry. If he was late home, his mum would be suspicious about where he'd been. Tucking the package firmly inside his top he jogged to Jade's house. When he reached the front door, Daryl was waiting inside.

'Kyle, man, good to see you again. Thought you'd decided against joining us.' He smiled as he handed Kyle a twenty pound note.

'Yeah, well, thought I'd just do one more delivery seeing as Jason needed a hand.'

'Brilliant, brilliant. To be honest, Kyle, we have a huge load of gear coming in tomorrow that all needs delivering. Are you up for it? You'll earn about £100 for the evening.'

A hundred quid? For working one evening? Kyle's mouth dried up. It sounded too good to be true and it probably was. But surely, if he just did jobs for one evening, earned a bit more money, he could stop? Couldn't he? He had only delivered two packages, and there was no pressure on him to deliver more, was there?

'Yeah, well, I'll have a think about it.'

'Yeah, yeah, sure. No pressure. There's a pile of work here if you want it, Kyle.'

The next day, Kyle went to the sports shop and bought the tracksuit bottoms. There, now he had a spanking new tracksuit. He looked cool in it. As he browsed around, he noticed the trainers, the trainers of his dreams – the latest Nike Airs! Much cooler than the Adidas that he had asked his mum to buy him. Wow. Kyle picked the display shoe up and held it; he wanted to stroke it. But at a price tag of a hundred and twenty quid, there was no way in this world that he could afford them. Reluctantly, he put it back.

Back home, Kyle hid the bag containing the tracksuit bottoms in his room upstairs. His mum would know that he had no money and couldn't afford the latest pair of trousers. What was she going to say when she found out that he had them? She would be suspicious. Kyle realised that he hadn't thought this through. He would have to keep them hidden until he'd come up with a plan. All night long, Kyle could not stop thinking about those trainers.

10th October 2019

Kyle glided along the path on his new bike. He felt a vibration in his pocket as his phone received another message. This meant one thing: another delivery. He looked at the message; it was a request for a delivery to a flat about a mile and a half away. Kyle yawned: he hadn't had much sleep.

His brand new Nike Air trainers forced the peddles faster. The reflective stripes on the bottoms of his Adidas sweat pants made silver circles as car lights shone behind him in the fading light of the dreary evening. Kyle steered onto the pavement and pulled his phone out of his pocket. He liked his new phone nearly as much as he liked the new bike that he'd been given. Of late, he had gone from feeling that he was just another non-descript kid in school to feeling like he was a cool person, with cool stuff that most of his mates couldn't afford. Kyle liked feeling part of something, something big, being rewarded for his efforts with money and respect. Kyle had never felt cool or important before.

After his first delivery, Daryl had given him a bit more work, delivering smaller packages to various addresses in town. Sometimes he had to collect larger ones from cars parked at inconspicuous locations. It had all seemed so easy at first. He started skipping school more often than usual to do deliveries. Initially he had been raking it in - once earning a hundred pounds in one evening. He wasn't stupid, he knew that some of the people that he was taking the packets to were known drug addicts. But soon, Kyle began to realise that his newfound wealth and the feelings of importance and belonging were ephemeral.

There were things that Kyle was beginning to find disconcerting. Over the last week, he had earned less than twenty pounds a day despite the fact that he was making countless deliveries. Mainly because Jason had left. Kyle had wanted to ask him why he had quit, but it was as if Jason had just vanished. He had gone from posting pictures of his new bike and trainers on Instagram and Facebook every day to posting nothing whatsoever for the past week. Kyle had sent him messages to ask him why? But the elusive Jason hadn't replied.

This weekend Grandad had asked him to go and watch Wrexham playing. When Kyle had told Daryl that he was going out on Saturday and he wouldn't be doing any deliveries, he wasn't very happy.

'What do you mean you're going out, Kyle?'

'Well, it's… I'm going out with my grandad.'

'Right, well, when you've been out with your grandad, you need to come straight back here. You're going to have to work later.'

Work later? It was Saturday!

'But I…'

'Don't lose me any business, Kyle, or you will be very sorry,' Daryl replied. His voice was cold.

Despite working longer hours and much harder for the gang, Kyle didn't seem to be getting as much respect as he once had.

'Stop flashing the cash, Kyle,' said one of the older lads when he noticed Kyle's new trainers.

'Yeah, come on, you prick, you'll end up drawing attention to yourself, and us, and that wouldn't end well, for anyone,' said Daryl.

Kyle didn't know where Jade was, but he hadn't seen her at the house all week. She had disappeared around the same time that Jason had. He was beginning to feel that Mo was right - something very odd and slightly sinister was going on.

As he cycled along the pavement to his next delivery, Kyle mulled it over. He hadn't been to school for two days. Strangely enough, Kyle missed school. He missed seeing his friends, and having a laugh. And he was tired; he had had no more than eight hours sleep in the last three days. His arms, legs and back ached from all the cycling that he had been doing.

'Where have you been all day?' his mum asked him angrily when he got home.

Kyle huffed. 'Out.'

She put her head in her hands.

'Kyle, are you going to tell me what the bloody hell is going on? You're out all hours, I've had the school on the phone saying that they're reporting me to Social Services again because you've been missing whole days of school! And what the hell are those on your feet!'

His brand new trainers! Kyle had forgotten to take them off before he had walked into the house.

'You've got new trainers, a new bike, a new phone, and you won't tell me how you got any of them or where they're from!'

Her eyes bored into him. Unable to meet her gaze, Kyle lowered his head.

'Did you rob them?'

Kyle managed to look up at her. He shook his head slowly. At least he wasn't lying… he hadn't robbed them.

'I bought them off a mate.'

'What with, Kyle? You haven't got any money!'

She stood with her hands on her hips.

'Well, come on, Kyle, answer me. Tell me, which of your *rich* mates are going to sell you a near brand new pair of a hundred and twenty pound trainers for the five or ten quid that you might manage to scrape together from saving your pocket money up? Which one is a secret millionaire's kid living round here?'

Kyle turned his head away.

'Do you think I'm stupid, Kyle? What are you doing? Robbing stuff? Selling drugs? Something worse? Where are you getting the money from?'

She was onto him. She had him backed into a corner. Kyle no longer enjoyed his job; the creeping around, the lying, the feeling that his life was spiralling out of control, and now social services. He had to sort himself out. But he had to get her off his back while he did it.

'Just leave me alone! What do you care? When did you ever buy me anything decent? Why don't you get a better job? Yours is just crap.'

Her face turned red with anger.

'What with, Kyle? I earn minimum wage, working my arse off so that I can keep a roof over our heads. Money I have for food and other things every week is less than those trainers cost!'

Kyle wanted to tell her, he wanted to. Instead of acting defensively, he wanted to come clean. But he couldn't. Daryl had made it very clear that if he found out that Kyle had told anyone, there would be trouble.

'I do that "crap job" as you call it, so that I can be here for you when you get home, except you never are now, are you? So don't you dare be so ungrateful!'

'Yeah… well, you… you don't give a shit about me, you… you haven't even told me who my dad is!'

Kyle barged past her. But as he did so, he accidentally pushed her into the wall. She tumbled backwards.

He stood still. His jaw dropped open as she lay crumpled up on the floor. Her mouth was quivering; tears welled up in her eyes and began to stream down her face. He wanted to pick her up, to hug her, to tell her that everything was going to be alright - but he couldn't do that. He had gotten into something big, something uncontrollable, something that was way out of his comfort zone, something he that knew he needed to get back out of, quickly. Eventually he spoke.

'S… sorry, Mum.'

She raised her head and looked up at him, composed, her eyes burning with a mixture of hurt and anger.

'I… I didn't mean to do that.'

She didn't reply for a while, she simply stared up at him.

'Why do you think that I never told you who he is, Kyle?'

He shrugged his shoulders.

'Have you ever thought that I'm trying to stop you from becoming him?'

Her words ripped through him like a knife and plunged deep into his heart.

'Screw this!'

Kyle stormed out of the house into the crisp evening air. He took a deep breath as a realisation struck him; his dad must have been bad, really bad. To think that despite all his mum's hard work and love, he, Kyle, was becoming exactly like his father, was a bitter pill to swallow. What was he doing? Who was he becoming? He had just pushed his mum over! It had been an accident, but she probably thought it had been intentional. He had to stop all this before it got any bigger, before he fell out with his mum, before he got into real trouble, or kicked out of school for good. If this was the way that his dad lived and this was what it was like, he got why she had never encouraged Kyle to meet him. Besides, Kyle had decided that this life wasn't for him. And he was tired. Tomorrow he would have a day off, start winding down and going straight. As he grabbed his bike and left the house, his phone pinged again: it was Daryl asking if he had made the drop and telling him to pick a packet up from one of the guys who transported the goods. This time it was Nathan, the guy with the orange BMW with blacked out windows and black alloys. Apparently, he fetched packages from Ellesmere Port on his way to and from work every day. Kyle would collect the packages hidden in the boot of his car from around the back of his house on the estate and transport them to Jade's house. No questions asked.

Kyle went to pick the packages up and headed back to Jade's house.

When he arrived, he parked his bike around the side of the house and went in. A new lad who had just started was about to go out on deliveries. He was much younger than Kyle. Kyle longed to tell him to stay away from the gang, to get out before he got involved any deeper, but he dared not to do so. There was only Daryl and Bert in the house. Bert didn't leave Daryl's side. He acted as his minder. Kyle had tried to talk to Bert, to make friendly conversation, but he gave flat, one-word answers. Kyle flaked down on the chair next to Daryl. His phone pinged again; it was a text from his mum. He felt in no mood to answer it. Instead, he threw the phone down onto the table in front of him and sank further back into the chair. Kyle was not looking forwards to this.

'Daryl, mate, I won't be in tomorrow.'

Bert continued his cold hard stare at Kyle. Daryl appeared nonplussed as he blew the smoke from the joint that he was smoking out of his mouth.

'Why's that?'

'Well, I haven't been to school for a few days. My mum's asking questions.' Kyle pointed towards his phone as it pinged again. 'She's onto me.'

Daryl put his joint down in the ashtray on the table and sat forwards to face Kyle. He leant so far towards him that Kyle began to feel intimidated.

'Well, you know we need you here, mate.' He put his hand on Kyle's shoulder. 'You're part of the gang now, you've got people relying on you; if they don't get their goods, they ain't going to be very happy, mate.'

Daryl paused. The silence was uncomfortable. Eventually he sat back in his chair, picked his joint up and took another drag before he blew the smoke out slowly.

'Do you know what I'm saying, Kyle? Mate?'

Kyle nodded and put his head back into his hands.

'Yeah, yeah, boss,' he replied. 'But school's getting twitchy. I'm already on report, got social services on my case, and if…'

'Thing is, mate, if the punters get upset, and have to wait, so do I, I get very upset, don't, I Bert?

'You do, Daryl,' replied Bert gruffly.

'Because, Kyle, people go elsewhere. That's bad for business.'

As he sat back, Daryl pulled out a box from the side of his chair and opened it slowly. Inside, Kyle could see large pieces of glinting metal. A feeling of overwhelming terror began to build up in him.

'It's bad for my business that I've worked very hard to set up,' said Daryl as he took a large knife out of the box, followed by a gun. 'And the more people leaving, the harder poor Bert's job is of making sure things go smoothly here, isn't it, Bert?'

'It is, Daryl,' said Bert, looking at Kyle as if he was going to murder him.

'And I can't let anyone, or anything, get in the way of that, do you know what I'm saying?' Daryl glared at Kyle through narrowed eyes as he gripped his shoulder.

His hand felt cold and hard. It was as if the grip of his hand was a metaphor for something else. Something uncontrollable that was sucking Kyle deeper and deeper into a mire from which he couldn't extricate himself. His throat began to dry and sweat poured from his forehead. If Kyle left, Daryl would easily find him, and then what would happen? Kyle's heart began to pound in his chest; he had got this wrong, so wrong. Why, oh why hadn't he listened to Mo?

Daryl inspected his knife closely, then he stared back up at Kyle coldly as he waited for his reply. Kyle was getting Daryl's message loud and clear; he would have to come back tomorrow, and then the day after that, and the day after that. Despite feeling more scared than he ever had in his life, Kyle remained composed and unflinching.

'OK, boss.' He forced a smile at Daryl. 'Leave it with me. I'll sort it.'

Daryl loosened his grip on Kyle.

'Good man, good man!' He brushed Kyle's shoulder down. 'I've got faith in you, Kyle, lots of faith, you won't let me down, will you?' He sat back in his chair, his eyes piercing into the very depths of Kyle's soul.

'I'm a reasonable guy, Kyle. I'm sure you can see where I'm coming from.'

Kyle forced another smile.

'Yeah, boss, yeah. I get what you're saying … I'll…I'll sort it!'

Daryl nodded at Bert. Bert walked over to Kyle and gripped him by the shoulders.

'Yeah, because you're in the gang now, you don't just leave. People that leave, nobody sees them again. They go missing. A bit like your mate Jason. Do you know what I'm sayin'?'

Kyle nodded slowly. He tried to speak, but he couldn't. The saliva in his mouth had long stopped flowing.

'Now, now, Bert. I don't think there's any need for that. Kyle understands, don't you, Kyle?'

Kyle nodded slowly.

'For sure, Kyle, for sure. Just one more thing, mate.' He pulled a package from underneath his seat and handed it to Kyle. 'Keep this safe for me till tomorrow.'

Kyle took the package in his trembling hands.

'Got it, boss.'

'Don't lose sight of it, Kyle, you keep it with you, at all times, 'til tomorrow.'

Bert loosened his grip of Kyle.

'Will do, will do, boss.' said Kyle as he began to walk backwards. 'Well, I, er…see you both tomorrow then.'

'Aw you definitely will.' Said Daryl menacingly.

Kyle turned and walked slowly out of the house. He wanted to move quicker, but he dared not, in case Daryl or Bert noticed that he was so keen to leave.

Kyle had never felt so petrified in his life. He had nowhere to go and no one to turn to. At least not anyone who, if he asked them for help, would not end in as much danger as he was in: he was trapped.

He wanted to go home, to see his mum and tell her everything, to say that he was sorry, to reassure her that he would stop and promise that he would never get into anything like this ever again. Then he wouldn't end up like his dad and she would be happy, and everything would be OK. But he couldn't tell anyone. If Daryl found out he would surely stab him with his knife. Or shoot him. Maybe Bert would just snap his neck with one twist. Kyle contemplated whether or not it was worth the risk, then at least that could be the end of it. But he doubted that it would be. The thought of staying was unbearable, the thought of leaving untenable.

Outside, Kyle filled his lungs with the cold, crisp October air. For a few seconds, he simply revelled in the fact that he was still alive. He needed a plan… fast. Kyle tucked the package into his coat and felt around in his pocket for his phone to reply to his mum. But his phone wasn't there: he had left it in the house! If Daryl was phoning and texting him, Kyle wouldn't be contactable, and that would make Daryl angry – very angry!

Cold chills crept down Kyle's spine as he realised that he would have to go back in and get it. He turned around, and walked cautiously towards the door. But just as he went to open it, he heard Daryl's voice through the broken pane of glass in the front door. He sounded like he was speaking to someone on his phone.

'Yeah, man, it's Kyle. He's gonna buckle. Told me he had to go to flaming school tomorrow, and he's under social services, so got the authorities all over him. Yeah, yeah, always a sign, mate. I've had to give him a bit of a warning for tonight.'

Kyle stopped dead in his tracks at the mention of his name. Whatever it was that Daryl was saying about him sounded ominous. Kyle listened hesitantly from behind the door, frightened to hear what Daryl was going to say next.

'Yeah, come up here tomorrow when he comes back in the morning, yeah, yeah, we ship him out for good to Hereford. Gave him the package, gonna get a couple of the other Bics to jump him tomorrow on the way to school so he'll think he's lost me the big money and goods.'

Daryl laughed cruelly. 'Yeah, still using the same original package!'

So that was why Daryl had given him the package to look after. He was being set up!

'No, mate, not to Brick Road, Jade and Jason are there and he knows them, to Beech street… yeah, mate, I know she looks like a rat, but she's making a bit of money for us there, we can keep her a bit longer before she just disappears as well.' He sniggered.

So Jade and Jason had been taken to Hereford! Miles away! It sounded like Daryl was pimping Jade out down there, but what had happened to Jason?

'Yeah, mate, we'll see Jason off next week, he's losing it, he's becoming a liability. Yeah, yeah, usual disposal method. We can put him in the boot of the car I got here and drop it in the quarry pool at the back of Oswestry; it's done its time, it'll be under surveillance from the pigs, saw an unmarked outside yesterday! Yeah, need to get rid, two birds with one stone and all that.'

Daryl and whoever he was talking to were planning to murder Jason! Talking about him as if he was a piece of meat, a mere commodity to just be used, worn out, and then disposed of!

'Yeah, Kyle can go to Beech Street, and if he moans or starts getting shitty, we get rid of him too. Na, no one will know where he's gone, na, he's just a Bic, mate.'

Kyle had heard the gang talking about "Bics" but he had never really understood what the phrase meant. It was when they were talking about people in a less than complimentary manner, usually about people that had done something to annoy or compromise the gang in some way. The last time that Kyle had heard the gang talking about "Bics" was when they were discussing Jason one day last week – the day after Kyle had last seen him. Now it all made sense! A sensation of impending doom engulfed him as a realisation began to dawn; "Bics" were plastic disposable pens, "Bics" were people like him, and Jason, and Jade, who were disposable, expendable, that didn't matter if they went missing or were never seen again.

'Yeah, mate… na, when he bolts, or pisses us off, he's dead. No one round here will miss him anyway, na, he hasn't even got a dad, mate…'

Kyle's blood froze. How did Daryl know that he didn't have a dad? He'd never spoken of his dad to anyone except Mo, least of all to Daryl or any other members of the gang. This implied something; Daryl had been checking up on him, investigating his home circumstances and his situation to ensure that he was nothing more than a "Bic" before luring him in. His heart sank as he realised that if he should just "disappear", only his mum and grandad would care, and how would they know where he was? His close friends would be too frightened to get involved. Kyle's blood ran cold as he realised that sooner or later he would have no further use to the gang.

'Yeah, mate, we need to wind it up here in the next week or so and move it on anyway, so yeah, we can take Kyle there...'

So when I'm no more use, I'm dead!

'OK, mate. Shit, got no baccy left. Going to the shop in a minute... yeah, yeah…'

Kyle crept back around the side of the house to where he had left his bike, praying that he wouldn't be seen. If Daryl suspected that Kyle knew what his plans were, he would surely execute them prematurely.

Kyle inhaled deeply to try and reduce the rate of his pounding heart. His mind raced through every potential way to escape from Daryl, but he kept coming back to the same conclusion; there was no way out! If he went back tomorrow, Daryl would send him to Beech street in Hereford where he would eventually meet his end, maybe in the quarry pool near Oswestry. If Kyle messed up or annoyed Daryl, he was dead. If he didn't turn up tomorrow and just went back to school or stayed at home, Daryl would find him and shut him up, making sure that he was jumped for the parcel. Whichever way he looked at it, sooner or later Kyle's time on this earth was up. Daryl wasn't going to just let him go.

Kyle pulled his bike up and remained around the back of the house, praying that Daryl wouldn't come around the side for any reason. Eventually he heard him, talking to Bert as they both walked out to his car together, and drove off. Kyle had to think, fast!

Kyle looked around at the rubbish in the back garden. He eventually found a plastic bag. He put his hand into it and used it to pick up the key that Daryl hid under the stone at the side when nobody was in. At least he knew that Jade wasn't there, but sometimes other people were; clients who took their drugs with the gang and then passed out upstairs in one of the bedrooms or downstairs on one of the chairs. There was only one thing for it.

He ran upstairs to do a sweep of the house to ensure that there was no one in any of the bedrooms then came back down to check the kitchen and bathroom.

Satisfied that the house was empty, Kyle returned to the lounge. The curtains were shut. Jade's house was messy and there were several flammable items within easy reach; piles of paper and cardboard, nail varnish remover, cooking oil, Vaseline. As he looked around in desperation for a lighter Kyle saw his salvation: the end of Daryl's joint burning in the ashtray. Kyle poured some of the liquids around the room and flicked the remains of Daryl's joint onto some paper doused in cooking oil which he then added to the pile. Fire began to rip through. He stayed for a few seconds to watch the fire take hold; the flames danced up the curtain and licked into the wooden furniture. Kyle watched the flames reach the plastic case of his phone on the wooden table.

As the fire ripped through the room, Kyle made a hasty exit from the back of the house. No one was around and none of the other houses in the immediate vicinity had their curtains open. He locked the back door, replaced the key, grabbed his bike and cycled swiftly up the path at the side towards the main road, throwing the plastic bag into a nearby bin as he did so. It was nearly half past seven. The main roads were at a standstill due to roadworks. As he cycled in and out of the stagnant traffic, Kyle realised that Daryl and Bert's journey would be somewhat delayed. He took a gamble and cycled to the nearest shop which was just on the other side of the main road. He reached the shop just in time, parked his bike outside and, as he went in, he saw them pull up in the car outside. Daryl got out of the passenger seat.

Kyle felt a fluttering in his chest as his eyes met Daryl's. For now, he would have to pretend that everything was normal, that he had no suspicions that something was amiss. Trepidation set in as he contemplated how this could all go so badly wrong.

'Alright, boss?' he said to Daryl. 'Was just gonna pop back to the house, left my phone.'

Daryl nodded and pulled his mouth into a cold half-smile. Kyle hoped to goodness that Daryl hadn't noticed how tightly his knuckles were gripping his bicycle handles, the sweat dripping down his forehead, the oil that he had spilled on his tracksuit bottoms, the smell of smoke.

'Sure, sure, Kyle, mate, you know how to open it, don't you?' replied Daryl condescendingly. Kyle nodded back up at him.

Daryl paid for his goods at the till and headed back out. Kyle picked up a can of coke and a Mars bar, paid for them and stood outside eating them, waving cheerfully to Daryl and Bert as they drove off. Feeling nauseous with every mouthful, his stomach in knots, Kyle waited. The seconds that passed seemed to take forever. He heard his cue... then he paused for a few more seconds just to make sure…

There was a definite wail of sirens in the distance, coming closer towards them. Fire engines, for sure.

He threw the remnants of his snacks into the overflowing bin next to him, jumped back on his bike and swiftly set off back to Jade's house. There were a myriad of ways that Kyle could take on his journey back to the house on the large sprawling estate; some were safer than others, some longer, some shorter. This time, he needed to take the most indiscreet route; he needed to be seen, his timing impeccable. He had to give Daryl his package back.

As he reached the corner of the street where the house was, Kyle looked down the road. The front of Jade's house illuminated the pitch black November evening as varying shades of iridescent orange and yellow flames licked out of the windows and up towards the sky. Thick smoke billowed into the air. Right on cue, there he was: Daryl's car was parked at the side of the road half way down the street, he was standing outside it, on the phone to someone. Kyle pulled up next to him as Daryl ended his call, his face pale.

'Shit, boss! The… the house!'

Fixated on the burning house and clearly preoccupied about what he should do next, Daryl didn't reply for a few moments. Eventually he spoke.

'You know nothing about any of this, open your gob to anyone, mention my name and you'll never be seen again, Kyle. Understand?'

'Sure thing, boss.'

Slowly, Kyle unzipped his coat, pulled the package that Daryl had given him out and handed it back to him. There was something else that Kyle no longer wanted.

'Give me the bike too, Kyle.' Kyle dropped his bike next to the car.

'Chuck it in the back, watch the gear.'

Kyle opened Daryl's boot, and put the bike in.

'Er, where's Bert?'

'Gone back to get the key for the back door. It's covered in prints. Now, get in the car, Kyle, you can come with us too.'

'No, Daryl.'

Daryl's eyes opened wider as he heard the sirens. Up until that moment, he had been oblivious to the wail of fire engines and police sirens that were fast descending upon the street. He stared hard at Kyle. The street was now beginning to fill with people who had noticed that Jade's house was on fire. The last thing that Daryl would want would be to draw attention to himself. If Kyle refused to go with him, it would be very silly of him to attempt to drag Kyle into his car, or threaten him with a knife or a gun.

Bert was walking back down the road towards them.

'I bet it was this stupid dick not putting his fag out properly. Well, he's gonna pay for this,' said Daryl. 'Mention my name, Kyle, and you're dead meat...'

'You got it, boss.'

Kyle waked off up the adjacent path towards the road. Moments later he heard a door slam and, under the faint street light, could just about see Daryl and Bert speed off with little time to spare before a fire engine and a police car came screeching around the corner. As he turned and watched the car disappear down the road, he let out a huge sigh of relief. The relief was ineffable: he had been given a second chance, at least for now. Maybe he would be back in a few days, a week or a month. But by then, Kyle would have had respite, enough respite to make a plan. Surely Daryl would never suspect him, not if he thought that he was going back to the house for his phone. Regardless, soon there would be nothing left for Daryl to come back for: the traces of his empire would soon be reduced to ash, everything would be gone: everything except for a dispensable "Bic" called Kyle.

Kyle made his way back home via the longest, most visible route possible, just in case he encountered any members of Daryl's gang who were expecting to steal a package from him. Possibilities of what might happen next raced through his mind. If the police spoke to him, he would deny all knowledge of the gang and accept whatever consequences awaited him. Punishment for keeping quiet could not possibly be worse than the circumstances that he had just managed to evade.

Kyle longed to do things; he longed to go back to school, to pick his old phone up and erase his social media accounts, to wear the inconspicuous cheap old trainers and his worn out tracksuit bottoms that his mum had bought him, to try hard in school and make everyone proud of him, but most of all to start over again. He looked down at his trainers. He had wanted them so much, now he hated the sight of them. Had it have been feasible for him to do so, Kyle would have handed them over to Daryl with his bike and the package and walked back home barefoot.

Kyle felt lighter than he had in weeks. When he got home, his mum was waiting for him at the door.

'Hi, Mum.'

'What the hell have you been doing and where have you been?'

Kyle shook his head.

'Nowhere, Mum, just hanging out with my mates. Anyway, I'm just off to bed. I've got school in the morning, got to get an early start.'

He took off his trainers and opened the cupboard at the bottom of the stairs. He placed his trainers on the shelf at the back, behind the junk, where he could not see them.

'Kyle.'

'Goodnight, Mum.'

Her jaw dropped. He kissed her on the cheek and walked upstairs. He lay down on his bed, and, before he knew it, he had drifted off to sleep.

11th October 2019

Kyle's alarm began to ring. He had had more sleep the previous night than he had had for the last few days put together, but he was still tired. Eventually, he managed to open his eyes, so disoriented that he couldn't even remember what day it was.

And then he remembered! There was no agenda, no phone to check, no expectation for him to go and do things that he no longer wanted to do. Despite the fatigue, he felt oddly refreshed. He felt like Kyle again; he had almost forgotten what that felt like.

He was free!

He got up, got dressed and looked for his school bag. It had been a good week since he'd bothered to take it to school and he had no idea where it was. He went downstairs and made himself a cup of tea. It was seven o'clock. He hadn't done any homework or been to school much since he had started working for Daryl so he was way behind on everything. Kyle went back upstairs and picked up his old mobile phone. He hadn't used it for ages and the battery was flat so he charged it up. Usually, he would have a look at his Facebook and Instagram accounts, but he had deactivated them all.

He knocked for Mo on the way to school. Mo opened the door. He grabbed Kyle tightly.

'Mo, man, I'm sorry.'

'Shit, man, I've been worried sick about you. Why didn't you answer my calls? I had visions of you dying in that fire at Jade's last night! I tried to call, but your phone just went to answerphone, and you've deleted your accounts! I couldn't find you on anywhere even on Instagram! Then I came round and you're mum said you had gone to bed.' Said Mo, incredulous.

'I was catching up on the hundreds of hours of sleep I've missed lately.'

'I told you it was dodgy, why…'

'How did I think I could do a couple of drops and leave… just slap me, man.'

'What happened last night?'

'Don't know.' Kyle shrugged. 'Looks like they've all done one though. I'd left before then.'

Mo stared hard at Kyle. Eventually he put his head in his hands.

'Woah, woah, hang on a minute, let me get my head round all this. Let me get this straight – I was worried sick that you've just died in a fire, when actually, you didn't, the house is gone, and you managed to leave your phone there so now they can't phone you? And you've gone off Instagram? And Facebook?'

'Well, er… yeah.'

'Mate, that all sounds really… lucky.'

'Yeah, I doubt that they'll be back round here, at least not for a bit. Gives me a bit of breathing space.'

'What makes you think that? How do you know they've not gone somewhere else?' asked Mo, suspiciously.

'Well, the gaff's gone... where would they go now? The police will be all over them.'

Mo didn't reply. Kyle could tell that he was finding his lucky break difficult to believe.

'Hopefully they'll leave you alone for a bit, but don't be surprised if they show up again. What's happened to Jason and Jade? Everyone's saying they've disappeared into thin air.'

Kyle shrugged. 'Dunno.'

He hated lying to Mo. He was the one friend that Kyle could trust. But if anyone came asking him questions, it would put Mo in an impossible position. There was no way that he could tell Mo about what had happened, at least not yet.

'You're gonna get bollocked in school, man. When were you last in?'

'The bollocking I'm about to face in school is gonna be nothing compared to what could have happened to me…it'll be worth every second.'

Mo shot him a knowing look.

Kyle knew that he would be in trouble in school and he didn't care. Part of him was looking forward to being sent to see the headmaster. That was the exact person that he needed to see. He needed to be straight and honest with him; he may even need his help.

'I'm getting my head down, this break and lunchtime; I need to start knuckling down, man, do well in some exams. Otherwise, I'm never gonna get out of this place.'

'I've been thinking the same. I'm just, well, worried about people calling me a square and all that like, innit?'

Kyle paused and looked up at Mo.

'I've just come this close to losing my life. I don't care who calls me a square from now on, they're welcome. Look, please don't ask me any more about it, Mo, I don't want to put you in a position if anyone comes asking anything.'

Mo simply nodded – he had seen all this before.

As they walked towards class, Mr. Hargreaves, the headmaster, was walking down the corridor towards them. He beckoned to Kyle.

'Kyle Joseph, come with me.'

'Later, pal,' Kyle said to Mo as Mr. Hargreaves led him off towards his office.

'How nice of you to join us, Kyle. I've got several missed days, with no accountability from anyone about where you were. Do you want to try and explain yourself before I suspend you?'

Kyle shrugged.

'Look, sir, I'm gonna be honest with you, and you're the first person I've told.'

Mr. Hargreaves's face dropped in shock. He wasn't used to Kyle speaking seriously, let alone sharing his secrets with him.

'Go on…'

'I got myself involved in some trouble on the estate. I couldn't get here.'

'Right… and are you still in this trouble?'

Kyle sighed. Mr. Hargreaves was used to hearing about such issues. He wasn't stupid, he knew exactly what Kyle was implying, that he had been involved with gangs, drugs, thieving or a mixture of all three and/or something else.

'I don't think so. Not at the moment.'

'Are the police likely to come knocking at your door?'

'I don't think so.'

The truth was that Kyle didn't know if the police were coming or not. The fear that he had of them hauling him off to the station to be questioned was nothing compared to the fear that he had experienced last night of the possibility of his life being ended. But one thing was for sure, he wouldn't be telling them anything.

'That's what they all say. Is this a matter that I need to refer to the police and social services?'

Kyle shook his head. 'Look, I've decided that I want to go on the straight and narrow now.' He looked Mr. Hargreaves in the eye, meeting his incredulous stare. 'I know you don't believe me and I don't blame you, but I want to settle down and get on. Please, please, sir, will you just give me one more chance? Can we make a deal or something? I'll hand all my GCSE coursework in by half term? Or, I dunno, go to the library every day? Just, please, don't suspend me!'

Mr. Hargreaves looked at him in disbelief. Kyle couldn't blame him for not taking him seriously.

'Well, Kyle, I've already had to phone social services about your recurrent non-attendance. I will be obliged to report concerns about you engaging in criminal activity to the police and I really don't think that I can just, "let you off". You need to prove yourself, Kyle. I'm going to speak to your mother because, if you appear here, in my office again, I will be looking at not only suspension this time, but full expulsion. Have I made myself clear?'

'Yes, sir.'

'And there are several conditions that I want meeting. Firstly, you will sit at the front of the class from now on, no messing around.'

'Yes, sir.'

'You will go to the library every lunchtime to study, instead of making your way down the field with the rest of your friends to smoke, which I know that you are still doing.'

'Yes, sir.'

'And I will receive no reports from outside of school from now on… concerning suggestions that you have been involved in illicit activities, or anything that you shouldn't be doing. Otherwise I will be phoning the police. Have I made myself clear?'

'Yes, sir.'

'Prove to me that you're serious, and I'll give you a chance.'

Kyle breathed in a large sigh of relief. He had never ever asked Mr. Hargreaves for a second chance before. Everything that he was telling him to do, Kyle needed to do anyway. He just needed a genuine excuse to be able to do it.

'You got it, sir. Look, if I don't turn up again, you can exclude me, but I won't let you down, sir.'

Mr. Hargreaves looked puzzled. He pointed his finger at Kyle.

'OK, Kyle, but like I said, any more piddling around, or not showing up, and you're for the high jump. I am, of course, going to need to speak to your mother about this…'

Kyle nodded. 'Of course, sir.'

It was inevitable that sooner or later, the police would come knocking at her door anyway.

'I'm glad that we both understand each other, Kyle, now you'd better get to maths, in the front if there's any room.'

'Yes, sir.'

Kyle left the office and walked down the corridor to maths. He was now fifteen minutes late. He sauntered in. Mo looked up at him and gasped in delight; he had been fully expecting Kyle to have been sent home. Kyle winked as he made his way over, high fiving some of his other mates as he did so.

'Got to sit down at the front, boys. Hargreaves has told me he's excluding me unless I do.'

'Kyle Joseph!' shouted Miss Pedreschi. She quite often sent Kyle out of the class to "study". 'How dare you walk in fifteen minutes late? And then come in and disrupt my class?'

'Sorry, miss, just had to go and see Mr. Hargreaves.'

'Well, don't come back disrupting my class! Either come and sit at the front where you will not be disturbing other students, or walk back out!'

The class paused as they waited for Kyle to leave the class, fully expecting this to happen as it was what he usually did. Kyle hated maths. He loved to leave the class and grabbed any opportunity to do so. Miss Pedreschi pulled out a chair at the front of the class as if to demonstrate that she was giving him the chance to stay. Perfect, he could sit there with no distractions. So instead of heading towards the door like he usually did, he walked up to the front of the class. He sat down in the aforementioned chair at the front. Miss Pedeschri's jaw dropped.

Kyle looked up at her, pulled his books out of his bag and put them on the table, as if he was playing a serious game of poker, and his books were his cards. A gasp went around the whole class.

'OK, Kyle, no messing around today. I'm glad, er, to see you've come to your senses at last! Yes, er so, trigonometry today.' She looked at Kyle suspiciously in between sentences as he began to take in the lesson and write in his book.

To everyone's amazement, Kyle did not flinch; he sat there and listened intently. Sitting at the front of the class enabled him to hear exactly what she was saying. The lesson was much easier to follow and with less stimulation and distraction everything seemed to make more sense.

Kyle could feel the anticipation in the class. Concentrating with this kind of pressure on him was hard. They were all preparing themselves for the same old story: at some point Kyle would mess about, get shouted at, and then be asked to leave. The whole lesson would be dragged out, and then once he had gone everyone who was interested (which was all of about five people) could finally get on with some work. After a while, everyone got bored of waiting.

After class, Kyle stayed behind.

'Er, miss, Mo told me you gave out some past exam papers the other day. Can I have a look? You know, to see what it is that I've got to learn?'

The teacher looked up at him in disbelief.

'What's happened, Kyle? Are you going to tell me? You haven't been off because you've had a brain transplant, have you?'

'Er, well, miss, I just want to get my head down and pass my exams.'

She fished around in one of the drawers of her desk and handed him some papers.

'What's happened, Kyle?'

'To be honest, I got into some trouble. It's made me have a long hard think about stuff! I need to get my head down!'

She looked up at him with a slight smile. 'I hope so; it's not before time is it, Kyle? These exams, they could be your keys to getting out of here and making something of your life. You've got to come to school, so don't waste the opportunity.'

'I won't, miss.'

Next it was break. Kyle found Mo in the corridor.

'Mate, I need to catch up on some of this work. Hargreaves told me I'm not allowed out at break and I've got to go to the library. You coming?'

Mo was hesitant. Kyle knew why; he didn't want to act like a swot, and end up getting picked on.

'Na, mate, I think I'll go and catch some of the others outside.'

'Fine, I just got to, you know, get my head down for the next few months. I'm in turd street otherwise.'

'Yeah, that's cool, man. Look, I'll catch you later, yeah?'

Kyle walked off in the direction of the library. He had never been in there before. It was empty. He sat down at one of the tables and looked around. It was a large room, full of shelves piled with books that looked as if nobody ever took them out to read.

He had English next. They were reading Shakespeare's *Macbeth*. He had only ever read the first few pages of it. Apparently, the class was up to the middle part of it. He took his textbook out and began to pore over what he had missed from the past few weeks. Fully expecting it to be deathly boring, Kyle began to read. It was a bit boring and it wasn't his thing really, but it was supposed to be related to real life. Kyle questioned how it could be related to real life when it was set in the fifteenth century. And there were witches? It sounded like a complete load of rubbish.

'Oi, there.'

It was Mo.

'Well, I couldn't just let you stay here on your own, could I?' he said as he pulled his books out and sat down. 'I just hope to god nobody sees me in here.'

'Cool, just starting looking over Shakespeare. Mate, it's all double-Dutch to me.'

For the next fifteen minutes, Kyle and Mo read over their English homework and made a list of the analogies that they could find with modern day life. When the bell rang, they were ready.

Kyle made his way into class and sat down at the front. None of his friends were in this class, so at least he didn't have any distractions.

'Kyle? Are you feeling OK?' Mrs Donovan asked.

'Er, yeah, why?'

'Well, it's just that you don't usually sit there, at the front.'

'Well, Mr. Hargreaves told me I've got to sit at the front, miss.'

Mrs Donovan looked at him in disbelief.

'Fine, but any messing about and you're out of here, OK?'

Kyle nodded.

She read out the text book, glancing occasionally at Kyle just to reassure herself that he was doing what he was supposed to be. Then the class read together. Kyle even replied when she asked him what he thought that one of the paragraphs meant and what the underlying message was. She told him that he was half-right. Kyle felt secretly pleased with himself. English wasn't Kyle's favourite subject, but the lesson wasn't as bad as he'd thought that it would be.

At dinner time, Kyle and Mo went to the canteen for their lunch.

'So, how was English?'

'Yeah, OK, you know the bit we did about the witches, well, she said that my comparison was spot on,' said Mo in amazement.

'Cool.'

Kyle stared across the canteen. Mr. Hargreaves stared back at him. Kyle nodded. Mr. Hargreaves nodded back.

'So are you going back to the library after this?'

'Yeah, I better had...'

'Look, don't tell anyone…' said Mo in a hushed voice, 'but I need to revise, I want to pass my GCSEs.'

'So do I. My mum's right, if I don't, then how am I ever gonna get out of this place?'

'Well,' said Mo in a low voice, 'can you just say I'm coming with you because I feel sorry for you? Because I don't want to leave you in the library on your own? Or something?'

Kyle nodded and began to snigger.

'Aw please, mate.'

They were shortly joined by some of their other friends.

'Kyle, mate, where you been?' asked Eddie.

Kyle looked up and smiled. 'Well, the gangs packed up and left, I've got nothin' better to do, innit? My mum's threatened to chuck me out unless I come back to school.'

'Shit, man, did you hear that Jade's house got burned down last night?'

'Yeah. From what I've heard, they've, shall we say, moved their operations, shipped out to another destination - I'm surplus to requirements.'

Mo's eyes burned into Kyle. Kyle could tell that he was beginning to suspect what had happened, and how Kyle had been able to leave the gang. He could almost hear the cogs turning in his friend's mind as he worked it all out.

'I've had a bollocking off Hargreaves. I've got to sit at the front of the class and go to the library every lunchtime from now on.'

A sigh went around the table.

'That's rash, man.'

'Crap.'

'Yeah, it is, but otherwise I'm excluded. I don't care', he continued, full of fake bravado, 'but my mum said she'll chuck me out.'

The truth was, Kyle felt relieved. Relieved that he no longer needed to act up, or make excuses, or pretend to be someone that he wasn't. He had an excuse to get his head down, there was no pressure to be cool, or fail in school.

'That's crap, man. You comin' down the field, Mo?' asked Eddie.

Mo paused.

'Er, na mate, er… me and Kyle are sharin' a fag, we're gonna do it quick behind the back of the school before he has to go to the library.'

'No worries. Catch you later.'

The others walked off.

'Sharing a fag behind the back of the school? I haven't even got any fags, I've kind of given up.'

'Me too, I haven't had one since last night. I'm quitting.'

They finished their lunch and returned to the library. They had a look at the maths past exam papers that they had been given. The mock GCSE exams were coming up in January. One of the teachers who had told Kyle in no uncertain terms that she would not be putting him in for his exam was Miss Pedreschi. Kyle decided to at least get his head down and try and convince her to change her mind.

That evening, walking home, Kyle's bag was heavy. It was full of exam papers and text books. As he parted company from Mo, there was someone that he had to go and see. Someone to whom he owed an explanation regarding where he had been for the past few weeks. Someone who Kyle needed help from to do one final thing to extricate himself from the gang. He knocked on Grandad's door.

'Grandad, please can I borrow your computer just for a second? I've got to type some stuff up for tomorrow for school and my printer wouldn't work last night.'

'Yes, sure, son, come in.'

Kyle went in and sat down on Grandad's sofa.

'So, how have you been?'

'Well, not great, to be honest.'

'Got yourself into something you couldn't handle?'

'Yeah.'

'I'll make us a brew.'

Kyle pulled up a word document, enlarged the font to twenty and quickly typed. He waited until Grandad retreated to the kettle, then printed the document out, pulled on some plastic gloves and slipped the paper into a plastic wallet. Then he printed out the address of the police station in town. The letter gave brief details about Jade and Jason, where they lived, where they had been taken to, and about what the gang purported to do to them.

Kyle just managed to slip his gloves off before his grandad came back.

'Oh ta, Grandad, it's just to, er, type the front cover for my maths.'

'Well, son, I'm glad to see you're settling back down to doing your work. Your mum's been worried sick about you, so have I.' He handed Kyle his cup of tea.

'Yeah, I know.'

'So what now?' asked Grandad.

'I need to get my head down now, go on the straight and narrow, and well, just make something of my life.'

'That's very profound, Kyle. Do you actually mean it? Or are you going to keep putting your mum through such worry?'

Kyle shook his head. 'No, never again.'

'So what is it you need to type?'

'Oh, er just to start an essay and type up a front cover for something…'

Kyle carried on typing. He had to write a five hundred-word essay for English about the weather and reflect on how it made him feel. He decided to start that. It needed to be in after half term. Maybe if he could get it done over half term and hand it in, Miss Donovan would put him in for his exam. Grandad made him another cup of tea and brought him some biscuits while he typed away.

'So, mate, what's happened to the bad crowd that you got in with? Because I'll be honest with you, bad crowds don't just come and go, once you're in them, you're in them...'

Grandad had lived on the estate all his life. His street was in one of the nice quiet areas. He made it his business to get to know people and he had a lot of friends there. He knew who was OK and who wasn't. He had seen the comings and goings, the various people who ended up in the mire. People he remembered as babies, who had had untimely deaths due to crime, drugs, and alcohol. The whole trajectory.

'Well, I didn't technically leave, they moved their operation to, shall we say, an alternative location.'

Grandad paused for a few seconds.

'Did it have anything to do with the fire at Jade's house?'

Kyle stopped what he was doing and looked up at his grandad. Grandad knew. Kyle nodded slowly up at him.

'Right,' said Grandad. 'So what now?'

Kyle shrugged. 'I don't know, Grandad. I'm hoping they'll have moved on by now.'

Kyle wasn't lying. He truly didn't know if or when Daryl and his gang were going to come back. He sincerely hoped that they wouldn't, but he had no guarantees; anything could happen. The only thing that he could do if Daryl did come back was to keep far away, as far away as possible from him.

'Well, if they do, you're going to have to move from round here. You're going to have to put a bit of distance between you and them. You're going to have to be inaccessible to them, so that it's more work for them to track you down, and they just let it go.'

Kyle nodded. 'I know, Grandad. I'd miss you and Mum, but I know, plus, it'd all be my own fault.'

'You haven't really come here to do your coursework, have you?'

Kyle shook his head.

'What have you come here to do?'

Kyle pulled on a second pair of plastic gloves and pulled out the plastic wallet from his bag with the paper in it. He showed it to his grandad.

'Kyle, what have you got yourself into?'

'Please, Grandad, don't say anything. I can't print it on my printer, it's got my traces all over it. I've put gloves on, so there's no fingerprints anywhere. I'm gonna put it in a stick down envelope when I get a stamp. They're in trouble down there, Grandad. I don't even know where they are, I just heard Daryl mentioning Brick Road and Hereford. It's all a longshot.'

Grandad took a deep breath in. 'So you're going to need a stamp. And ideally to post the letter before the last post?'

Kyle nodded.

'I'm gonna have to go and buy one, and post it.'

'Don't bother, I've got one here. I'll go and do it.'

Kyle shook his head. 'No way, Grandad, what if it's got any of your prints on it? Or you leave a trace somewhere? What if they trace it back to you? This is my mess.'

'So what happened with the fire?'

Kyle didn't reply for a few seconds. 'Jade and Jason went missing. I heard the main guy Daryl on the phone to someone, Grandad, telling them I was becoming a liability because I wanted to stop working; he was planning to take me to Hereford and make me work from there. He said Jade and Jason were already there, that he needed to get rid of them, and when I got too much…'

'You'd be next,' replied Grandad. He stood up slowly. 'I won't ask you anymore, Kyle, leave your gloves on and don't touch anything.'

He went outside. Kyle could see him opening his garden shed. Soon he returned with a pair of plastic gloves.

'Pass me that paper.'

Kyle shook his head. 'No, Grandad.'

'Give it here.'

Kyle passed Grandad the plastic wallet with the note, the printed label for the front and a brown envelope that he had taken from the desk in the library in school. Grandad tore a few strips of Sellotape off and discarded them, then he opened the wallet and carefully taped the address to the envelope. Once he had done so, he placed it back in the plastic wallet.

'Right, what are you actually doing now?'

'Er, my coursework.'

'OK, I'll go and get a stamp, then post this, don't worry, I won't touch it.'

'No, Grandad, you can't. What if they find out it was you?'

Grandad knew exactly what help Kyle needed and what to do about it.

'They won't. Just promise me, you'll never ever get involved with anything like this again.'

Kyle shook his head. 'Never! Thanks, Grandad.'

The following evening when Kyle went home, there was a knock on his front door; it was the police. Kyle had been expecting them.

'Kyle Joseph?'

'Yeah?'

'We need you to come down to the station; we need to ask you some questions about something.'

Kyle's mum gave him daggers by the door. Kyle shrugged.

'Yeah, sure.'

****

Kyle sat down at the interview table at the police station with his mum.

'So, Kyle, do you know why we've brought you here today?' asked one of the policemen.

Kyle looked down at his feet. It was undoubtedly to be questioned about his involvement with Daryl and the goings on at Jade's house. To deny everything would be futile. Undoubtedly CCTV would crop up somewhere of him making deliveries or going to the house. But maybe the police didn't know as much about Kyle as he worried that they did? Eventually, he shook his head.

'No, not really.'

'For the benefit of the tape, Kyle is shaking his head. So, Kyle, it is because you have been seen going in and out of the house occupied by a lady called Jade Robertson. A house that was commandeered by a gang, a house where there has been illicit activities going on, mainly, the dealing of illicit substances.'

Kyle could feel his mum's eyes burning into him.

'Is this true, Kyle?' she asked.

'What? I only dropped off a few packages for them. I don't take drugs! I don't know nothing about illicit activities.'

'Oh my god!' said Kyle's mum as she put her head into her hands and placed her head between her legs. 'Are you stupid, Kyle?'

Kyle admitted to delivering a few packages, but denied knowing anything about them. Because he was still fifteen, technically he was still a minor, a victim of Daryl and his gang, a pawn in the bigger picture of the crime that was being slowly unravelled by the police. His mum looked at him with disappointment and anger as he replied to some of the questions.

'So, come on, Kyle, we know that you were delivering packages for the gang, and we know that you were at the house last night. And you are telling me that you didn't know what was in the packages?' asked the detective.

'No, sir,' replied Kyle.

'But you must have known some of the people that you were taking them to?'

'Yes, sir.'

'So, are you telling me you had no idea that the packages contained drugs?'

'Well, no, sir. They seemed like a nice group of people, I just wanted to help them out.'

'So who were these people, Kyle?'

'Well, one was called Donald Duck, another one was…'

'Don't play the fool with me, Kyle,' said the exasperated detective. He stared long and hard at Kyle.

'Kyle, I know you know what was in those packages. You're scared, aren't you? Scared that they're going to come back. Well, it's OK, we'll give you protection.'

Protection? Yeah, Kyle had heard all about "police protection". They would promise him the earth until they got what they wanted then they would throw him straight under the bus.

'Yeah, I'm sure you would,' replied Kyle, sarcastically. One thing he wasn't doing was grassing anyone up or mentioning any names - everyone knew what happened to grasses.

'You were seen at the house, the evening before the fire.'

'Yes, I did a delivery.'

'Where to?'

'I can't remember, sorry.'

Daryl had told Kyle to never, ever reply to any messages that were sent to the phone. If the police had the records of the numbers, it would be quite clear that they could be messages that could be sent to anyone.

'We'll be checking your phone, Kyle. We'll find it, Kyle.'

'Yeah, no problem, feel free,' said Kyle, handing over his old phone, the one that he hadn't really used since before he had started working for the gang.

The police officer stared hard at him.

'I know you'll have had two phones, Kyle, where's the other one?'

'What other phone?' said Kyle, shrugging his shoulders. 'I don't know what you mean.

The two detectives looked at each other, dismayed.

'Do you like to write letters, Kyle?'

'Letters?'

'Yes, letters, and send them to the police?'

'Naa, never been very good at English. Don't even know if I'm getting put in for my exam...'

'Yes, you flaming well are, Kyle,' said his mum.

Kyle could tell that they knew that he was lying. As hard as they probed, Kyle remained steadfast and did not slip up.

Reluctantly, they let him go and advised him that they might be contacting him again.

'How could you be so stupid?' his mum said, almost hissing at him as they got outside. 'I brought you up to be a good person, how could you let me down like this?'

Kyle didn't reply; he looked down at his feet.

'I wish they had charged you. I wish you had been taken off me, if you're going to be putting me through this every time you want to earn a few quid! I'm obviously doing a really bad job!'

'Mum, I'm… I'm sorry. It all seemed so easy, and chilled. I didn't know it was going to get that intense, or I'd be in that amount of trouble. Before I knew it, they were pressuring me to stay and do more… Mum, you've got to believe me.'

'Well, either it's over, or next time I'm phoning social services. I'll put you in care myself. Seriously, Kyle, drug dealing? You'd be safer in care or young offenders than you would be staying living with me.'

'I hope you would, Mum, but I promise, it's over.'

Kyle's heart dropped at the thought of his mum sending him into care. Never had she spoken to him in such a manner before. 'I'm sorry I let you down; I'll never do it again.'

As Kyle and his mum walked back home, they came to a section in the road that had been cordoned off by the police. Two police cars with flashing lights had pulled over a bright orange BMW with oversized wheels and blacked out windows. Kyle recognised it; it was Nathan's car. As he looked closer, he saw that Nathan was being handcuffed by two police officers. It was at that moment that he noticed Leanne sitting in the passenger seat next to him. Kyle pulled the hood of his sweatshirt up and ducked his head as he and his mum crossed the road. Leanne had texted him twice in the last few days asking him to meet her at her house. Kyle had not replied, partly because he had had his old phone switched off and partly because he had had more important things to think about. At one time, he would have jumped at the chance to go round to Leanne's. But looking at the company that she was keeping, Leanne was in trouble. And trouble was something that Kyle was very keen to avoid.

20th October 2020

For the rest of the term, Kyle got his head down just like he'd promised everyone that he would. The realisation that he had come so close to losing his life coupled with the fact that he felt so ashamed at letting his mum and grandad down had prompted him to persevere. Plus, Kyle figured that if he spent his time studying, it would keep him out of trouble.

'I just don't get it,' said Mo, as they walked home from school.

'What?'

'Those equations they're telling us about.'

'Na, to be honest, I didn't at first, but I think that I do now. Do you want to come round and I'll show you?'

Mo grinned up at him. 'Yeah… I mean, it's too cold and dark to go down the park with the others anyway,' he said unconvincingly. It wasn't that cold.

'Mum, Mo's coming to study.' Said Kyle as he walked into the house with Mo.

Kyle's mum was making tea.

'Oh, hi, Mo. Are you staying for tea?'

'Oh yes, er, what are you making, please, Miss Joseph?'

'Cheese and onion pie with chips and peas, you're OK with that, aren't you?'

'Yes, please.'

Kyle's mum was a good cook. Kyle knew that Mo liked coming for tea. She made him more than he had at home and he always devoured it. Kyle felt that she knew that Mo had it hard at home and liked looking after him.

'So what are you learning today?'

'Er, equations,' said Kyle.

Kyle and Mo tried to work through them. They still didn't quite understand the more complex ones, but grasped the basic concept. When they went to maths tomorrow, they would feel more prepared.

Even though he had covered ground, there were still several outstanding pieces of coursework that Kyle had not done. It all felt overwhelming. But he ploughed on through and got it all done, slowly. He had until after half term to complete everything. On the Thursday evening before the Friday deadline, Kyle had nearly finished. He sat up late as he waited for his mum to read over the work that he had done so that he could make his corrections. There was just his history coursework that he hadn't yet started. He doubted that he was going to be put in for the exam anyway, but he had promised his mum that he would try his best. There was only one thing for it!

Kyle stayed up, furiously writing, then going over it again and again until his eyes began to shut. Each time he felt his lids closing, he got up and made himself another cup of coffee and carried on. He had nearly finished, he just had to read through it to make sure that it read right. The next time that he saw his mum, she was getting up for work. He was almost done.

'Kyle, what on earth are you doing up this early? Where are you going?'

'Nowhere, Mum.'

'Then why the hell are you up at this time? Don't tell me you've stayed somewhere you shouldn't have? Or you're going somewhere? Have you stayed out all night? Please don't tell me that…'

She was still suspicious; she constantly questioned him about what he was doing. He could tell that she felt that his newfound keenness to attend school was some kind of a cover up for something else. Despite the fact that of late he had given her no reason to doubt him – the more that he got his head down and got on with it all, the less she seemed to trust him.

'I haven't been to bed, Mum. I've been doing my history coursework. It's due in today.'

'Really?' she asked, her eyes wide. 'You've stayed up all night? To do that?'

'Yeah, I promised you.'

'I thought that's the one you'd sacrifice, having done the rest and worked so hard. I wasn't even going to mention it. But you've done it anyway?'

'Well, I've done something…'

'I'm proud of you, Kyle,' she said. 'Let me have a look at it.'

'But you'll be late…'

'I don't care.'

His mum read through Kyle's work before she left and made some points for him to change. She was definitely going to be late for work.

'Aw, I'm never late, once won't hurt. It looks OK, just a few typos to change; you've got more than enough time to do it and print it off again.' She hugged him tightly as she left. 'I'm proud of you, Kyle.'

Kyle felt all warm inside. He did his corrections and printed his work off. Then he had a shower, packed his things and made his way into school, feeling faint with tiredness, his eyes aching in the morning sun. Earlier than class started, Kyle went in to speak to Mr. Hussain, his history teacher.

'Sir, I know you think I'm a waste of space, and you don't plan on entering me for the exams, but, just in case you change your mind, I've done the coursework.'

Mr. Hussain looked up at him.

'I'm impressed, Kyle. I've noticed that you've been working harder lately."

Kyle nodded. 'Thank you, sir.'

'If you're not interested in doing the work, Kyle, then I'm not interested in teaching you. But I'll have a look at your coursework, and we'll see. I can't say fairer than that, Kyle, OK?'

'OK, sir,' said Kyle as he took his place at the front of the empty class.

As the day wore on, Kyle felt increasingly tired. By the time that he got to his maths lesson at the end of the day, the daylight was stinging his eyes and his whole body felt as if it was going to collapse.

'Kyle, can I have a word?' asked Miss Pedreschi after maths.

'Yes, miss.'

'What's wrong with you today? You look unwell! As if you're not concentrating. I notice that over the past few weeks, I've hardly heard a peep out of you and you've been getting your head down. Then you come in today, and you look like you've been out partying all night. What is going on?'

'It's just, I was up late, miss, finishing off my coursework, for history. I haven't been to bed.'

Her face broke into a grin. 'I'm impressed, Kyle. Just to let you know, your change in attitude has been noticed, not just by me, but by your other teachers. You'll be sitting your maths GCSE.'

Kyle grinned to himself. 'Thanks, miss. I have worked hard, I'm trying. I won't let you down.'

'I know you have, Kyle. We all realise that. Now do me a favour? Go home, and get some sleep.'

'I'll be fine, miss.'

As tired as Kyle was, there was no way that he was going home to get some sleep. He was going out with Grandad to watch Wrexham play, and nothing was going to stop him from doing that, not even being tired. But before then, Grandad was taking him to Shone's café for a fry up – and their fry ups were the best. After a few cups of coffee, Kyle would be fine again.

29th October 2019

It was half term. Kyle felt as if his whole body was going to crash. He needed a break; a break from studying, a break from doing things all the time, a break from life. Plus, he wanted to spend some time with his friends - he hadn't seen much of them lately. Even though he felt proud of himself, Kyle longed to feel normal, with no pressure. The pressure of feeling like he had to prove himself was beginning to get to him.

Tonight, some of them had arranged to go to the cinema to see "The Joker". Kyle had stayed in that much and studied so hard that he still had money unspent from when he had worked for Daryl's gang. It was Mo's birthday. After the cinema, Kyle planned to take him to the diner. Kyle was looking forwards to just doing something normal with his friends, and then taking Mo somewhere for a treat, somewhere where they could talk about things other than their schoolwork.

When Kyle and Mo arrived at the cinema, to his dismay, Leanne was there.

'I think Leanne's still got a thing for you,' whispered Mo.

'Yeah, I was wondering. To be honest, mate, I'm not interested anymore. Plus, she was seeing one of guys from the gang.'

'Yeah, I know. I heard he got caught with twenty grand of coke in his boot.'

Kyle shook his head.

'Shit, Mo. What was I thinking?'

'Dunno. But if I were you, mate, I'd keep away.'.'

'Kyle, I'll sit by you,' said Leanne as they walked into the cinema.

'Er, sorry, I'm sitting by my main man Mo. I need him to cuddle me if I get too scared.'

Leanne looked put out. Kyle hoped that she would take the hint. Sadly she didn't. If anything, it made her more determined. One advantage of going to the library was that Kyle had managed to avoid her for the past few weeks. But the more that he refused her advances, the keener she seemed to become.

After the film had finished, everyone prepared to leave. Kyle was awestruck. "The Joker" was like no film that he had ever seen before. It wasn't like a Marvel movie. It was gritty, and real. It showed how easily a person could become subsumed in depression, and anxiety, and be downtrodden by society. Somehow it felt like there was an analogy between the film and his recent experience with Daryl. Except that he had been elusive, and nobody knew how he had resolved his personal situation. And Kyle could never tell anyone.

'Aw Kyle, I'll let you walk me home,' said Leanne.

'Na, sorry, I'm taking Mo to the diner, it's his birthday today.'

'Really?' she asked, looking put out. 'A private dinner together…'

'Come on then, sweetie, let's eat,' Kyle said to Mo.

'Ooh, yes, darling,' replied Mo.

They skipped off together towards the diner, leaving Leanne and her friend Vicky to walk home with the others. They entered the diner and went to the counter. Seconds later, to Kyle's dismay, Vicky and Leanne entered. Thinking quickly, Kyle deliberately took a seat at a table that was just for two people. Vicky and Leanne sat at the table next to them.

'Yeah, we felt hungry too,' said Vicky.

Kyle looked over at the menu above the counter. He noticed that Roxanne, one of the girls from school, was working in the kitchen area. Kyle didn't know Roxanne very well, she was one of the members of the gothic gang. Her hair was dyed purple and her lip was pierced. Roxanne had had several altercations with Leanne in school. These were usually instigated by Leanne making bitchy comments about Roxanne's appearance. Different and alternative, Kyle had always thought that Roxanne was kind of cool. There was another girl from school called Cornelia working behind the till, a quiet girl who Kyle had never spoken to. Both Roxanne and Cornelia were in Kyle's maths class.

'I'm shattered!' Kyle heard Roxanne say to Cornelia. 'All that studying last night has caught up with me. I can't keep my eyes open, then working here… ah well, at least we haven't got long.'

Cornelia nodded. 'Well, if you want some help, me and some of my other friends are planning to meet up in the library at break and lunch time to go over stuff, you know, for the exam. Why don't you join us?'

Kyle had seen Cornelia and her friends in the library. They got their heads down and talked about clever stuff. Sometimes if he and Mo were studying the same topic, he would try to listen in to see if he could get any tips and hints.

Roxanne laughed. 'Na, I don't think it's my scene,' she said. 'Besides, I'm really thick compared to you lot.'

Cornelia shook her head. 'No, it's honestly not like that, none of my friends are really clever, nor am I, we just work hard. Really clever people don't need to be sitting in the library on their lunch breaks studying.'

Roxanne paused.

'Come on, give it a try, you're obviously struggling at the moment, you need to try something else.'

'OK. I'll drop by at lunch time when we get back to school.'

Kyle noticed Leanne staring at Roxanne. He wondered if they were going to have another altercation. He hoped not; all he wanted was a quiet meal with his friend and for Leanne to not be there.

'Aw, look who's here. The weirdo with the piercings, and the biggest swot in school. Talking about studying in the library, how sad!' said Leanne loudly.

Leanne was starting already. Kyle looked over at Cornelia; she was leaning over a book on the counter showing Roxanne something.

'Right, maths, page eighty-two, equations.'

This was exactly what Kyle wanted to learn about. He strained to listen as Cornelia took Roxanne through the equation, step by step. She explained it clearly.

'But, but, that's easy!' said Roxanne.

Cornelia nodded.

'It is, when you just break it down.'

'Break it down, why haven't I thought of that before?'

'Yeah, like chunks, you'll never remember that whole page, just six or seven points.'

'So forget all the crap and padding in the intro about what you use it for?'

'Yes, basically,' said Cornelia. 'Just concentrate on the bits in between.'

'Sad ass!' said Vicky.

Hearing her, Roxanne and Cornelia looked up.

'Aw god,' said Roxanne, turning around. 'Here they are…'

'Oh great! And which lads are they with tonight? Aw, Kyle and Mo,' Cornelia replied.

Kyle attempted to ignore the friction bubbling in the restaurant and walked over to the counter to give his order to Cornelia.

'Yes? What can I get you?' she asked politely.

'Oh my god,' said Leanne loudly, pointing towards Roxanne. 'The hair!'

Kyle turned around to see what the commotion was. Roxanne's face looked like thunder from behind the counter. Cornelia didn't flinch, she remained calm and composed.

'What can I get you?' she asked again.

'Erm, one cheeseburger and chips and…'

Kyle was interrupted by Roxanne.

'I'm going to flatten her in a minute,' she said loudly.

'Sorry, I couldn't quite catch that,' said Cornelia.

'One cheeseburger and chips, and one…'

'Aw, look at Kyle, stuttering,' said Leanne. 'What's wrong, Kyle? You got the hots for the swot of the year?'

'Leanne, can you shut up? I'm just ordering my dinner.'

'Are you actually going to order anything? Or just sit there making sarcastic remarks?' Cornelia asked Leanne.

'Well, what if I am? What are you going to do about it?' replied Leanne. 'What's the matter? Is the library shut tonight?'

This was getting ridiculous. Leanne, for whatever reason, was just being rude and obnoxious.

'What do you think I do most lunchtimes, Leanne?' Kyle asked, turning around to face her.

'What? Go to the library? Yeah, only because Hargreaves told you to.'

Once again, Leanne began to insult Roxanne's hair. 'I mean, what on earth has she done to it? It's like a bush.'

Kyle turned around again. 'Leanne, just leave her alone. What's she done to you? She's just doing her job.'

'What? Are you saying that you like the dragged through the hedge backwards look?' Leanne said. Vicky sniggered next to her.

'I wouldn't say it's my style, but I definitely think that it's cool.'

Leanne laughed. 'Are you joking?'

Kyle looked over at Roxanne; she looked as if she was having to stop herself from marching up to Leanne and punching her straight in the face.

'So do you actually want anything to eat or drink?' asked Cornelia, looking up at Kyle as she waited to take his order. 'Because it has now taken three attempts and you still haven't managed to order anything.'

'Yeah, I do, a veggie burger for my good friend Mo, a cheeseburger for myself, two chips, a coke, and a Fanta.'

Cornelia pursed her lips. 'That will be nine pounds, please.'

Kyle handed Cornelia the money. She took it off him, opened the till and gave him his change.

'Well, she's managed to take your order at last!' said Leanne. 'What a waste of time all that studying is, working here.'

Kyle opened his mouth to speak. But before he could say anything, Cornelia beat him to it.

'Yes, I do *work,* and I do study, because I'd like to make something of my life, not end up as thick as pig shit, with my only aspiration being able to afford to go to the tanning salon with my benefits money or what I get from my drug dealer boyfriend, when he's not in jail, that is.'

Clapping could be heard from behind. It was Roxanne. 'Well said, Cornster, you tell the stupid wench!'

Kyle sniggered as he stood at the till. Cornelia turned to him.

'And what are you laughing at? What is actually funny, Kyle? Maybe if you spent a bit more time in school, and less time selling drugs to people and being a general knob-head, you'd actually be able to string two words together.'

Kyle stopped laughing. She said he couldn't string two words together! How dare she? Was that really what she thought of him? That he was someone that was so thick that he couldn't even speak properly?

'How dare you come down here with your classy girlfriend to insult us when we're just trying to do our jobs.'

'Whoa, whoa,' said Kyle putting his hands up. 'You've got me all wrong, I'm not thick, I don't deal drugs, and that is *not* my girlfriend!'

Cornelia shook her head. 'I don't think that I have. I don't know why you bother going to the library, you're not even going to be put in for any exams the way you're going, never mind pass any.'

'I'm gonna pass my exams, all grade C or above, you'll see.'

Cornelia looked back up at him.

'Yeah, whatever, Kyle.'

Roxanne began to snigger behind her.

'I will.'

'We'll see about that, won't we, Kyle?'

Kyle smirked at her. 'Oh, you certainly will...'

By now, Leanne had stood up, irate.

'You starting? Who you calling thick?' She pointed at Roxanne. 'I'll flatten you…'

'Yeah, whatever.'

Hearing the commotion, the restaurant manager came rushing out.

'Roxanne, Cornelia, what on earth is going on?'

'She started it,' said Roxanne, pointing over to Leanne.

'I… I… certainly did not,' replied Leanne. 'They started being rude to me and my friend here.'

The restaurant manager looked at Vicky and Leanne and then back at Roxanne and Cornelia.

'Girls, you need to apologise to these ladies, immediately.'

'No chance, she started it,' said Roxanne, pointing to Leanne.

Kyle had had enough. He had come out for a quiet night with Mo, and this was how it had all ended up. He just wanted some peace and quiet.

'I... I... I didn't! Did I, Mo? Kyle?' said Leanne.

Kyle looked over the counter at Cornelia and Roxanne. Apart from calling him thick, and a drug dealer, to be fair, they were only doing their jobs. Cornelia stood there with a concerned expression; Roxanne just looked mad.

'Actually, yes, you did, Leanne. You've been skitting them both since you got here. For no reason. Yeah, you did start it. So I'm not gonna just stand here and let them lose their jobs because you started on them, sorry.'

Leanne's mouth fell open.

'B… b… but.'

'So there you go,' said Roxanne to the restaurant manager.

'Roxanne!'

'What? Can I get on with my job now?'

The manager nodded. 'Well, if that's the case, I think that you'd best leave my restaurant,' he said to Leanne.

'Yeah, well, who wants to eat here anyway?' Leanne said.

Vicky got up and followed her out. Kyle breathed a sigh of relief. Thank god they were gone, now he could settle down with Mo and have a half-decent evening. Roxanne walked after them and opened the door. Out of earshot of her manager Kyle heard her hissing to Leanne as they walked out.

'Monday after half term, me and you, down the field…'

'You'll be very sorry…'

He and Mo sat down. Shortly after, Cornelia came over with their meals.

'Veggie burger, cheeseburger and chips, coke and a Fanta?'

'Yep.'

'Thanks, for that.'

'No problem,' said Kyle loudly, 'even if your mate over there called me a drug dealer, with bad taste for a girlfriend.'

'Yeah,' said Roxanne who began scrubbing the table next to them. 'You're not so much of a dick after all, are you?'

'No, and I don't sell drugs, Cornelia, at least not anymore.'

'OK, well, sorry for being judgemental,' said Cornelia.

'And I do like your hair, Roxanne – I think it's cool.'

4th November 2019

It was the first maths lesson after half term. Kyle sat at the front feeling refreshed after his break. He caught Roxanne's eye as she walked into the class. She gave him a slight smile. Cornelia was sitting two seats away from him at the front. And then Kyle realised something else. Leanne – when she turned up to school - was also in this class.

'Hi,' said Roxanne to Cornelia. 'Good weekend at the bike show?'

Leanne could be heard tutting loudly behind her. 'Yeah, great weekend with all the other weirdos at the bike show…'

Roxanne looked behind her at Leanne.

'Yeah, maybe I should have gone and sniffed some of my boyfriend's coke, oh sorry, he hasn't got any has he? Been arrested, hasn't he?'

'Yeah? Well wait til he hears what you've just said, you're dead meat…'

'Ooh, I better go and change my knickers. Tell him I hope he gets out early for good behaviour…'

'Come on, Rox, just leave it now,' said Cornelia.

'No chance! Me and her, down the field later. Can't wait…'

'Yeah… I'll… I'll… flatten you when we're done in here,' replied Leanne.

'I can't wait.'

'Rox,' hissed Cornelia. 'What are you doing? Just leave it.'

'I don't care. I can't wait to flatten her.'

The lesson began. Nobody was paying attention. Everyone was waiting with bated breath. It was quiet, so quiet that a pin could be heard dropping. After a protracted session, the lesson drew to a close, the class on tenterhooks. As Miss Pedreschi left the room, everyone procrastinated over putting their books in their bags, pulling their coats on, leaving the room. They were like fans addicted to a soap opera that couldn't wait to see what happened next.

'Come on then, bitch, get your sorry fake ass down the field,' said Roxanne to Leanne.

'Yeah, yeah, I'm coming, now, you freak,' said Leanne.

'In fact, I can't be arsed waiting to thump you down the field, let's take the corridor out there instead,' said Roxanne, indicating to the door of the classroom.

Leanne was beginning to look uncomfortable. Realising that she had an audience and needed to retain her status as someone who was hard, she swung her arm into Roxanne's face. It was a slap - a very soft, unconvincing slap. But she was clearly trying to get the first punch in.

'Is that the best you can do?' asked Roxanne. She started laughing, softly at first and then harder and harder and harder before she swung her fist into Leanne's face. Leanne stumbled around in a daze as Roxanne shoved her into the chairs behind her.

'Come on, get up, I even let you take the first shot, hard girl…'

Leanne got back up, looking dazed. It would have been an ideal opportunity for Roxanne to hit her again, but she didn't. Instead, she stood still, cool and calm.

'Y…y…yeah?' said Leanne, chancing her luck and trying to make a grab for Roxanne's face.

Roxanne shoved her backwards again and she fell in a heap on the floor. Kicks from Roxanne's heavy Doctor Martens rained into Leanne's ribs as Kyle flew over to Roxanne, grabbed her around the waist and picked her up, dragging her away from Leanne who lay coughing and spluttering on the floor.

'Get off me!' Roxanne said to Kyle.

'No, stop it, I'm not letting you go. You're going to get into trouble.'

Hearing the commotion from up the corridor, Miss Pedreschi appeared at the door.

'What is going on here?'

Kyle dropped Roxanne on the floor. She didn't speak. Leanne tried to get up.

'I… I… it was her, she hit me, s… she started it…'

Miss Pedreschi looked at Roxanne aghast. 'Roxanne, is this true?'

'Yeah, because she hit me first.'

'Is that right, Leanne?'

'I… I… I didn't…'

'Yes, you did,' said Cornelia.

'Ah, Cornelia, someone I can get some sense out of. You'll tell me what happened.'

'Leanne hit Roxanne in the face first; she was only defending herself, miss.'

'Is that right, Leanne?'

'N… no, she started it, for no reason.'

'Right, all three of you, school office now.'

****

'And you, you come here,' Roxanne bellowed after Kyle as he and Mo made their way over to the library the next day. 'What were you doing interfering? Why did you grab me off her?'

'Well, because I thought you were going to half kill her.'

'You should have let me at her; she had it coming!'

'Are you having a laugh? You pummelled her as it was! Any more and you'd have knocked her out, and got yourself into some serious trouble! You should be thanking me!'

'He's right, Rox, he probably did you a favour,' said Cornelia.

'Yeah, well, I could have got another smack in to the side of her face. A few more seconds and I could have given her another few good boots!'

'Well, I'm glad you didn't. I don't think she'll be starting on you again soon,' said Kyle.

'Yeah, well, I got a nice afternoon off. Pedreschi marched us all off to the office, sent me and that dick Leanne home for the day and that was it.'

'Well, I'll look forward to the next encounter,' said Mo.

'Oooh, 'encounter', that's a big word for you, Mo…'

'Yeah, well, we've been studying, haven't we, Kyle?'

'We have, Mo,' Kyle replied, looking over at Cornelia as he did so. She looked at him with incredulity. 'In fact, that's where we're going now, to the library to study some more, isn't it, Mo?'

'It is, Kyle.'

'Why? Because Hargreaves told you to go the library? Or actually studying?' asked Cornelia.

Mo and Kyle didn't reply.

'I hear no denial, Cornelia. I think they like it really,' said Roxanne.

'Me too,' said Cornelia. 'Fair play.'

They walked in the direction of the library together. Kyle and Mo sat at one table, Roxanne and Cornelia at the table next to them. It was otherwise empty except for the haughty librarian who sat behind the desk noisily eating her sandwich. Mo opened his text book.

'Yeah, all these "x" and "ys", I just don't get how they make that…' Mo said, complaining.

'I know, I think I get it, but then no.'

Kyle and Mo sighed. No matter how many times they looked over equations, they couldn't seem to understand it once it got a bit more complex.

'I just don't get it,' Mo complained again. 'If that goes there to make that, then what happens to that?'

Cornelia turned her chair around to face them, listening intently. 'Well, you've moved that to there, and if that is there, it must be the sum of these.'

When she pointed out the logic of the equation, Kyle half understood what she meant. But not quite.

'Come again?' said Kyle.

'Well, you have this, and you have to see what this is, so the only thing you can do is move that there, that cancels that out there, so what are you left with?'

'Well that's easy, x squared?' said Mo.

'Yes, and that's right.'

'Yeah, thanks,' said Mo.

Kyle put his pen in his mouth and smiled at Cornelia, watching her as she sat down. He was beginning to understand.

'Sorry, I don't get it totally, can you just explain one more time, please'.

'Well, if you move this there, and that there,' she began to explain, 'then that has to be the answer. There's no other logical explanation.'

'I think… I get it,' said Mo, looking up at Cornelia with undisguised admiration. 'Wow, are you like a genius or something?'

'No, it took me a while to learn, but I get it now.'

'Yeah… thanks,' replied Kyle. 'So, Mo, that means we can do the next page.'

Cornelia turned back around. Once they understood how to do it, Kyle and Mo had become engrossed. Neither of them dared to admit it, but after the break, they both emerged from the library feeling like finalists on University Challenge. If they could work out clever stuff like this, there was little else they couldn't do. But it was nothing that they could boast about, not in school, not to their other mates… it just wasn't cool.

Kyle and Mo followed Cornelia and Roxanne out of the library. Roxanne was in Kyle's design and technology class. She was the only girl there. They walked together as Mo and Cornelia parted ways to go to their respective classes.

'So why have you decided that it's time to get your head down, Kyle?' asked Roxanne.

'Honestly?'

'Yeah, you've gone from being the class clown, to the class swot in less than a month.'

Kyle recoiled in horror. Never before had he been referred to as a swot. It was in direct opposition to everything that he, Kyle Joseph, usually stood for. He wasn't a swot, was he? Maybe he was now. If he carried on like this, and Roxanne and Cornelia had noticed, it wouldn't be long before other people started noticing.

'Well, I got myself, er, in some trouble. It made me decide, I don't want to live like that anymore.'

Roxanne nodded. 'That's cool.'

Kyle nodded. Yes, it was really. Even though he was now a swot, and didn't want anyone else to know, he was secretly quite proud of himself.

'Thing is, I quite like having this quiet life. School ain't such a bad place when you know what it is you're doing.'

'I hate school, it's a shit storm. Half these other people? They don't know what life is. Or they've got no aspirations above this. Once school is over, if you want to do something with your life, you'll never see them ever again.'

Kyle laughed.

'You're probably right. And that's a good analogy about school, you see, I've been reading and everything, analogy, is that the word? When something is like something?'

Roxanne nodded.

'Anyway, you don't give a toss. You've always been, well, different to the rest of us, and not afraid.'

'Yep, while all the other girls were having pony parties and making glitter pictures, I was begging my dad to take me to rock concerts. I've got my crew of other misfits, except for Cornelia, she's just normal. I can't stand some of the other girls in this year.'

'Well, maybe they think you're weird; besides, you got trust issues, sister.'

Roxanne sighed. Kyle suspected she was probably right. Bullying in that school for being different was rife, especially from girls such as Leanne and Vicky. But Roxanne had a very hard outer shell; she was brave and dared to be different.

'Yeah, you're probably right, it's not easy fitting in when you're a square peg in a round hole. People just don't get me. And then I don't trust them.'

'Well, what about your family? Do they accept you?'

'Well, to be honest, I live with my mum and sisters. None of them are like me. So I tend to spend most of my time round at my dad's. He's into rock music and bikes like me.'

'That's cool. It must be cool to have a dad,' Kyle said with a sigh. He had spoken aloud before he could stop himself.

'Er, yeah, don't you see yours?'

Kyle shook his head. 'I don't even know who he is. The rest of my family say he's a bad guy. The only thing I know about him is that he's white not black. That's not very helpful.'

'Well, sometimes it's not a bad thing. If your mum has done a good job of raising you without him, and if she's a sound person, she must have a reason for skitting him.'

'She is sound, she's great.'

'Well, you know, the picture that you've got in your head of him, that might not be the same thing that everyone else is seeing.'

'I'd just like to know who he is.'

They had nearly reached class. Kyle realised that he had spoken to Roxanne more about himself and his inner feelings than he had to anyone for some time. He only really spoke to girls that he fancied. He didn't fancy Roxanne, and he didn't think that she fancied him. But he could talk to her. He felt comfortable in her presence. She was different, non-judgemental.

'Anyway, I'm sitting down the front. Why don't you come with me? I made a deal with Mr. Hargreaves that he won't suspend me if I keep my head down and sit at the front of the class. Come on, we'll learn more there. Just don't tell anyone, OK?'

'OK.'

Roxanne and Kyle sat at the front of the class. They listened, then they planned what they were going to make for their GCSE project, and worked hard. Roxanne said that her dad had loads of tools and bits in his shed that they could use to put the finishing touches in once they'd made it.

'Rox?'

'Yeah?'

'Please don't tell anyone that I want to pass my exams, will you?'

Roxanne shook her head. 'Only if you don't tell anyone that I do.'

1st December 2019

'Mum, I've been thinking.'

'Yes, Kyle?'

'I'd really like to, you know, know who my dad is.'

His mum stopped washing the pots and turned around to face him.

'Really? Where has this come from?'

Kyle shrugged. 'I dunno, I just would. I just want to know who he is, where I came from, what he looks like.'

His mum did not speak for some time. 'I knew you would, one day.'

'Who is he?'

She took her rubber gloves off and came to sit down at the table next to him.

'His name is Chad, Kyle. I don't know where he is.'

'Well, where is he from?'

'Here, originally.'

'Well, if you know that, how come you don't know where he lives?'

His mum paused. 'Well I don't know where he lives now, but last I heard, he was in prison. Again.'

There was a long pause. The pause was filled with the implication that Kyle's dad was not somebody that he should aspire to meet. Eventually, she spoke.

'I can find out where he is if you really want me to. But I don't want to be involved in any part of you meeting him, OK? And I certainly don't want to see him.'

'Why?'

'Well, Kyle, it's because he wasn't very nice to me when we were together. And he's not a good person. He's got worse, not better, over the last few years; he doesn't do great things for a living.'

His mum rarely bad mouthed anyone.

'You don't like him, do you?'

'I just never want to see him ever again, Kyle. So please, like I said, if you ever meet him, don't ever bring him here. And remember, you've just worked hard to get out of one lot of dire trouble, you don't need to be getting in any more.'

'OK, Mum, all I want to do is know what he looks like and who he is.'

'I know, I can understand that, Kyle. But at the moment, I genuinely don't know where he is.'

Later that day Kyle went into town to get his mum and his grandad Christmas presents.

'I don't want anything, the best present that I could have would be if you get your head down and study,' his mum had said.

Kyle looked at the Pandora bracelets in the shop window. His mum would love one of them but he couldn't afford one. He wondered if he could stretch to a charm? As he continued down the street, he noticed a familiar figure walking towards him. He knew that he should just walk straight past and pretend that he hadn't seen him, but Kyle felt compelled to talk to him.

'Jason. How you doing?'

Jason had his hood up. Startled, he stopped abruptly. Seeing that it was Kyle, the petrified look on his face subsided. He appeared jumpy.

'Yeah… yeah, er not bad. You?'

'Yeah, I'm fine, ta. Haven't seen you for ages, where have you been?'

Kyle knew exactly where Jason had been.

There was a long uncomfortable silence as Jason and Kyle both looked down at their feet. Kyle looked back up at Jason and studied his face closely. He looked haunted, trapped, as if it had taken him all of his energy just to be able to get up and walk up the high street, edgy, as if he was existing mainly on coffee, cigarettes and his nerves.

'S… so, is Jade OK?'

'Er… yeah. She's moved to one of the flats the other side of the park now.'

Another awkward long silence.

'Good… that's good. I heard her house burned down.'

'Yeah.'

There was a long pause. Eventually Jason spoke in whisper, as if he could hardly bear to say the name…

'You heard from Daryl?'

'Daryl? No.'

Jason's eyes widened at the very mention of Daryl's name. Kyle could tell that much as he didn't want to talk about him, he too needed reassurance that Kyle had not heard from Daryl - that Daryl was as far away as possible.

'You?'

'Er no, not since Jade's house burned down.'

'They reckon that was a set up. By a rival drug gang. They reckon they got to Bert somehow and he started the fire…'

Jason's eyes were wide. He looked haunted, as if he fully expected Daryl to appear around the corner at any moment.

'Th…they wanted to kill me, me and Jade. Th…they were planning to put us in the boot of a car. Then they… wanted to put Bert in the car first for starting the fire, but then the police came. They managed to arrest everyone, everyone except Daryl, nobody knows where he is.'

Arrested everyone except Daryl? Nobody knows where he is?

Kyle's heart stopped beating for a few seconds as Jason's words resounded in his ears.

So where was Daryl?

Kyle didn't reply, not daring to speak in case Jason shut down and stopped telling him things. Although part of him didn't want to know anymore, the other half of him was dying to find out more. But eventually, Jason, realising that he had probably said more than he should, fell silent. Eventually Kyle spoke.

'I've had the police at mine, asking questions.'

'What did you tell them?'

'Nothing.'

'No, me neither. They're charging me with drug dealing, told me they'd let me off if I spilt the beans. It's more than my life's worth.'

Jason shifted around uncomfortably. Kyle secretly thanked god that he was under the age of sixteen when he had been involved in the gang.

'To be honest, I was looking to get out anyway; he didn't seem keen for me to go though.'

'Sorry, I, you know, got you involved. It just all seemed so easy at first, like, money for nothing.'

'Yeah, I know.'

'Anyway, you've had a lucky escape. If he saw me now, he'd want to shut me up. I've seen it all, I know too much.'

So this explained why he was walking around town with his hood up, looking ashen, as if he had already met his maker – Jason was looking over his shoulder waiting for Daryl to reappear at any second.

'I think he will one day... just got to keep your head down, man, you and me both.'

'Well, he's on the run. He's got nowhere to go.'

'If he gets desperate, he'll turn up somewhere he knows, somewhere like here.'

Neither of them spoke as they mulled it over.

'If you see him, will you let me know? Just so I can split?' asked Jason, his eyes wide.

'Yeah, same here, man.'

Jason nodded.

'Anyway, take it easy for now,' Kyle said. Jason nodded as they parted company. He pulled his hood closer around his head as he walked off down the street. Kyle watched him go, walking quickly. How much power Daryl still held over him was apparent; he was paranoid, and quite rightly so. Jason was looking over his shoulder every two seconds. Although he was enjoying the peace, Kyle was well aware that he had left a can of worms buried somewhere in the ashes of Jade's house that could be forced open at any time.

He walked aimlessly around town for a while, just thinking. After he'd bumped into Jason, Kyle had almost forgotten about why he had gone there in the first place. He had the grand sum of thirty-two pounds and twenty-eight pence left to buy his mum and grandad Christmas presents. He decided to leave it until he was in the mood for shopping. Instead he headed over to Roxanne's dad's house - they were going to make a start on their project.

As he turned up the street, he noticed a man covered in tattoos cleaning his motorbike on the drive. Rock music blared from out of the front window of the downstairs lounge. Kyle knew he'd found the place.

31st December 2019

Kyle had enjoyed Christmas. He had spent the day with his mum and grandad. Then on Boxing Day his aunt, uncle and cousins had come to stay at Grandad's for the week. It had been great fun. Kyle didn't see much of his cousins, but they were sound. They lived in a large house on the coast of Devon. Kyle, Mum and Grandad were planning to visit them next year as they hadn't been able to do so last summer. For the time in between, he had met up with Mo, and sometimes Roxanne and Cornelia to study. Kyle had found this incredibly helpful and at last, felt that he was starting to get his head around everything.

Today was Kyle's birthday. His mum had taken him and Mo to a pub for dinner. As it was New Year's Eve, some of their other friends were going into town tonight. Mo was skint and Kyle wanted to study as soon as he got up the next morning. Neither of them wanted to admit it, but they didn't really want to go anyway. Instead, they had decided to pool the few pounds that they had to buy some beers. It was a clear evening; they had climbed halfway up the mountain on the other side of the estate. They sat, wrapped up in their coats, swigging lager and proclaiming their hopes and dreams for the next year, watching the fireworks being let off as 2020 started.

'What a year,' said Mo. 'If someone had told me that I'd be spending most of my spare time in a library this time last year, I'd have laughed.'

'If someone told me that I'd have nearly been kidnapped and forced to work for a county lines drug dealing gang, I'd have laughed.'

'That's true, man.'

'I wonder what we'll be doing this time next year.'

'Dunno, but I've got to get out of this place man.' Mo's face was serious.

'Why?'

'It's going to ruin me if I'm not careful. I just feel… it's dragging me down.'

'Why?'

'It's like, I don't exist. It's like they don't know me.'

'How do you mean?'

'My mum said the other day she can't wait for me to get a job and pay some keep. I know she's struggling, but the thing is, I don't want to get a job, not yet. I want do something, to be someone.'

'Well, what do you want to do? Like, what would you want to be if you could be anything?'

'I don't know, I don't know what I want to do, but I know what I don't want to do, I don't want to get involved in crime with Dad and Shashif, then go to jail, then come back out, then go back in.'

Kyle didn't reply, he just listened. Mo didn't often talk about his family. Best to let him vent.

'While they're in jail, she's putting pressure on me to get a job. Then when they come out, they'll put pressure on me to do something dodgy with the promise of hitting the big time, except I won't, it'll end in disaster.'

'Look, Mo, you're not your dad or your brother – you never were and you never, ever will be. Your dad should be looking after your mum, not you. You can't spend the rest of your life feeling guilty, compensating for him.'

'I know. Plus, the way my family are, I've come to realise, it's just not normal. Look at your mum, how hard she works, and your grandad. They've never been to jail. It's almost like, in my family, it's… normal.'

'OK, I get you don't know what you want to do, but what else do you want out of life?'

'I… I don't know, I think having a family and being there for them, paying for my kids, being around to see them grow up, living somewhere nice, that's not filled with drugs and dog shit.'

Kyle looked up at Mo. He had the greatest admiration for his friend. He wondered if his mum realised what a special son she had. How much he had his head screwed on? What a forward thinker he was? His potential.

'You know you having to stay in at lunchtimes? I might not have said, but I was really happy after that first time I came to the library with you, when we sat learning stuff, and it felt better in class after, like I could understand stuff.'

'What? You mean you didn't want to come and sit in the library with me?' Kyle replied with a hint of sarcasm.

'Yeah, that was the whole point, the first time I came, I came because I felt bad for you, but after that, I enjoyed coming. Not having to pretend that I liked smoking down the field, and getting into trouble.'

'I know, it was the one good thing that came of it all. I dunno about you, but I feel OK about the mocks.'

'Yeah, me too.'

'Look, man, you don't have to decide what you're going to do. You just have to decide what you're not going to do. We've done OK at sticking to it.'

'I just know they're going to pressure me.'

'Your mum's got a lot of problems, it's not easy for her. All we can do is get our heads down, work hard; if we pass our exams, we can think about it after. If you've done well, you'll have every reason to go your own way.'

'I wish my mum was more like yours,' said Mo.

'What? Bringing you up with no dad?'

'Well, yeah, like I love my dad, but he's been in jail for half of my life. I feel like I hardly know him. He might as well have not been there. He just comes out of jail, gets back involved with the gang, then goes back in.'

'Yeah, but what about the rest of your family? I'd love brothers and sisters.'

'We all get lost in that house. There are too many of us. On top of each other. She's too consumed in her problems to care about any of us.'

'Well, what about your dad?'

'When he's not in jail, all we do is spend our time hiding, worrying that someone's going to fire bomb the house, or about some drug gang that wants revenge. To be honest, I'm always relieved when he goes back in.'

Kyle sighed. 'Mate, it's mad, you don't know what goes on in someone else's head, do you? Me? I feel bad for not appreciating my mum when I should have. I've always felt envious of you having a dad when I haven't got one; I never realised that it was like that for you.'

'Mate, feel lucky. If he's anything like mine, he's not worth having. I hate myself for saying that, but it's true. I wish sometimes it was just me and my mum, so she'd have time for me. She doesn't know me, she's always too stressed trying to run the house, and dodge the bailiffs, and worrying about the others who do give her trouble.'

'Yeah, but it's like you're different to everyone else, Mo, not just your family, but in the school. It's like you've got a gift, Mo, a gift for seeing things for what they are, for seeing what's going to happen. You listen to your heart and do the right thing. You'll go far. Just trust yourself, carry on being yourself, because you're top, man.'

'So will you. If you can get out of the mess that you were in a few months ago, you can survive anything'.

'Exactly, and who was the person who tried to tell me what was going to happen? And that was exactly what happened? You were.'

They sat in silence for a bit. Eventually Mo spoke.

'You torched it, didn't you?'

Kyle's silence spoke volumes.

'That was epic, man. I had nightmares, about someone finding you dead, shot in the back of the head in the park and ending up on a slab in the mortuary.'

'It was a random, lucky break, Mo, that I'll tell you all about one day when I know no one's coming looking for me and it won't put you in a dangerous position. Anyway, for now we're just a pair of geeks.'

Kyle started to laugh. So did Mo. He was right, they were a pair of geeks.

'Everyone else is in town, partying, and we're sitting up a mountain, swigging cans and chatting shit about the future.'

'Hey, you've been deep tonight, Mo, I like our deep chats. You needed to get it off your chest. Saddest thing is, there's nowhere else I'd rather be.'

'Me neither.'

16th January 2020

Kyle had been entered for all of his GCSEs and, according to his teachers, and mainly because of his change in attitude, was on course for some reasonable grades.

His first mock exam was maths - the one that he dreaded the most. He opened the paper in trepidation, his heart knocking inside his chest. He looked at the questions, they were doable. Before, when the teacher had given him the past papers, they had seemed like a foreign language. Kyle had felt that he was learning Double-Dutch. Now, they just seemed like another page in a text book, familiar. Not as overwhelming. Slowly, he began working through the questions, finding them easy at first, easy to answer, and move on. The further he got into the paper, the harder they became. Once he had finished them, some of the harder ones began to play on his mind. He had to keep going back, and checking that he had done them right. Then he came to the last section. Equations.

Kyle worked through diligently, checking, and double checking his workings. Eventually, he finished. He checked the section again; no, it was definitely what he thought. And again… yes. Then he went back. He found a couple of mistakes, and rectified them. No sooner had he gone back to check for a final time, than the five minute warning came. Feeling that he couldn't look at his work any longer for fear of his eyes seizing up, he put his pen down and left his work on the table. He had got some wrong, he knew he had. But he had no more capacity to concentrate. Besides, most of it was OK.

'Well?' said Roxanne after the papers had been collected and they walked out together.

'Not too bad.'

'No, me neither. I had a good go at that equation section.'

'Much easier than the first time we practiced in class,' said Mo.

'That was hard,' said Eddie. 'I couldn't do most of it…'

Eddie had always declined their offers to study with them. Sensing that he had struggled the most, they turned the conversation to something else before going home to do some more revision.

In between exams, Kyle spent his days holed up in his room revising alone, and his evenings revising with exclusively or a mixture of Mo, Roxanne and Cornelia. When he reached the point at which he could no longer stand revising, he went for a run, or a kick around at the park with whoever was around for an hour or so to clear his head.

The penultimate exam was English. They were asked to read a poem and answer questions about it, and then write a short story about summer. English was the subject that Kyle found most difficult of all. He studied the poem; it seemed to be about a goose flying away. But the goose was an analogy for something else. Kyle felt that it was for escape, for leaving. He used some of the big words that he, Mo and Roxanne had learned the definitions of because they had read that they were in the curriculum, plus some analogies. Then for the second part, he wrote a story about the magical summer that he had just had at the lighthouse by the ship with his grandad. He felt that he had done his best.

Kyle managed to finish most of his work before the teacher gave them the five minute warning. He wrote most of his final paragraph and ended with a question of "what if?" Kyle meant to say what if he had never been, but on reflection he felt that that was a good as any place to end it.

24th January 2020

It was the last mock exam. The unusually sharp January sunshine shone through the tall window of the exam hall. The five minute warning went – Kyle was nearly done. There. A minute later, the final bell went. That was it, time was up. Kyle took a deep breath as he put his pen down. Had he done enough?

After, there was a house party at Norman Rowlands's house. Norman lived on the street near Jade's old house. The whole year was invited to his party. As they neared the house, the music could be heard from down the street. Norman lived with his dad who often worked away. He didn't seem to care if Norman had parties or not.

'What do you reckon, we've got an hour before someone calls the police?' said Kyle.

'Yeah, maybe a bit longer, depends on if the neighbours are working or not,' replied Eddie.

They looked around the street. Every other house was boarded up. Needles and broken bottles littered the floor along with dog excrement.

'Doesn't look like it,' said Kyle.

'Wow, Jade's old house looks grim,' said Eddie. Mo gave Kyle a knowing glance.

It did look grim. The windows and door had been boarded up. Around the windows the brickwork was blackened with smoke. The house was cordoned off with steel fences that had been broken down some time ago. Apparently the council were planning to start work on it in the next month or so. Chills began to travel down Kyle's spine as he thought back to that night and how wrong everything could have gone.

'I wonder what really happened to the house that night? It was weird it burned down after she'd gone to Hereford,' said Eddie.

Kyle caught Mo's eye and the slight smile on his face. They stood looking at the house for a few moments, before continuing to Norman's.

Norman's house was already full of people from school; they spilled out into the garden. Even though it was January, the afternoon sun was bright. Kyle felt a hand on his back.

'So, Kyle, where have you been? I haven't seen you for weeks. You still off your Facebook and Instagram?'

Leanne.

'Yeah, not bad, thanks. Just been at the library, you know, because they said I had to go there.'

'What? Still?'

'Well, yeah.'

'Ahh, so that's why you've been hanging around so much with that freak Roxanne. And your little swotty friend Cornelia.'

He went to walk past her.

'You've got bad taste, Kyle. Seriously, what have they got that I haven't?' He could smell the alcohol on her breath.

'Well, we all want to get on in life, so we've all got quite a bit in common...'

Leanne looked up at him, her face like thunder. 'What, like I don't?'

She turned on her heels and walked out of the room just as Roxanne, Cornelia and their friends turned up. Sure enough, it didn't take long for a commotion to begin in the front room.

'Yeah? Well you should just get out of here, you freak.'

'Why? Who are you anyway?'

'This party isn't for freaks. Look at the state of you, with your hair.'

'Well, at least I don't look the same as every other person that you follow on your crappy Instagram account. Anyway, if you've got a problem, let's step outside, and we can happily resolve it there.'

Leanne was obviously drunk, and she clearly felt invincible.

'Come on then, you and me, outside, now, come on, hard girl, let's step outside… now. I'll just batter you all over again like I did in school the other week!'

Cornelia grabbed Roxanne. 'Come on, Rox, just forget about her, she's just drunk.'

'What did you call me?'

'Leanne, you're not hard, you're drunk. You're just a waste of someone else's air. You know as well as I do that if you go outside with Rox, she'd rip your head off. Come on, Rox, don't let her rile you.'

'Whatever, you swotty little freak,' said Leanne.

'Well, if she's too shit-scared, I'm just gonna have to drag her out…'

'Rox, no, leave it.'

Kyle decided that this was as good a time as any to intervene in the situation.

'Guys, guys, just calm down. This party is for everyone. There's loads of room here. Why don't you just keep out of each other's way if you don't get on?'

'Yeah? Well, as usual, that fake-tanned plastic bitch started it.'

'Freak, no one wants you here,' said Leanne.

'You don't speak for everyone, Leanne. Rox is my mate, she's cool, I want her here,' said Kyle, putting his arm around her.

'Well, who cares? Maybe you could go home, and take your swotty girlfriend with you as well.' Leanne pointed to Cornelia.

'Now, now, Leanne, just coz I knocked you back, look, don't be bitter. I'm sure you'll find someone who finds your attitude and personality, I dunno, appealing, maybe?'

People began to snigger with Roxanne laughing louder than anybody else. Kyle wasn't sure if anyone else noticed the tears that welled up in Leanne's eyes. He felt sorry for her.

'I'm going. This place is full of freaks!' she said as she stormed out. Roxanne looked up at Kyle and smiled.

'Don't look at me like that, she started it.'

Kyle put his hands up in protest. 'I ain't looking at you like anything.'

'Anyway, who needs my gob when I've got you and your riposte?' she said.

'My what?'

'One of those big words you taught me the other week in English, efficacious comebacks.'

Kyle laughed. 'Efficacious, I used that in my English essay. Come here.' He hugged her. 'You know I just don't want you getting done for GBH and ripping her head off.'

'I don't care, I'd love to rip her head off.'

'Now calm down.'

Mo and Roxanne went to sit outside. Roxanne had borrowed her friend's guitar and started teaching Mo how to play. The alcohol was beginning to make Kyle feel woozy. After a while, he realised that he, Mo and Eddie were more than half way through the alcohol that they had bought. He had probably had enough. He went outside to join Mo, Roxanne and her gang. By now, Mo was playing a few chords.

'Wow, man, you're really doing your thing.'

'Yeah,' said Mo. 'I've not played before.'

'Well, now we might have a bit of time, can we do music night? Instead of studying for a few months,' said Roxanne.

'Yeah, I always wanted to play the drums,' said Kyle.

Everyone was having fun, the mood was jovial. The crisp January sun shone down on them, everyone was happy. They had been there a good two hours before, in the distance, a wail of sirens began to move closer and closer to the house. Ahh, now that brought back memories. Kyle remembered the last time that he had listened out for sirens in this area of town. He still couldn't believe that he had managed to pull that stunt off. Now, he was enjoying life while he could. Everyone began to down their alcohol and hide the bottles and cans in bins, behind bushes, and scattered around Norman's house. Shortly after, a police car pulled up outside.

'OK, OK, let's break it up shall we?' said a police officer as she emerged from the passenger seat of the car.

'Better get out of here before she realises that we're all leathered,' said Mo. 'I'm gonna go, I feel wasted.'

'Me too, brother.'

Kyle and Mo headed off home. As he got halfway home and bid Mo goodbye, Kyle began to feel as if he couldn't quite walk properly. The bright sun was hurting his eyes. He was only about a quarter of a mile from home. He retreated into one of the entrances to an alleyway to sort himself out for a minute and slumped down, feeling extremely drunk. He only had another few streets to go, he felt so tired. Kyle not only was drunk, but he looked drunk. He decided to continue to make his way home via the back streets and alleyways of the estate in an effort to avoid anyone who may be hanging around and try to take advantage of him or try to rob him.

Kyle burst in through the front door just as his mum returned from work. Smelling alcohol on him, she tutted.

'Kyle, what the hell have you been doing?'

'I got drunk, Mum,' he slurred. 'It's the last day of my exams… I wanted to have some fun.'

He collapsed on a heap on the sofa. Laughing, his mum put a blanket over him and fetched him a cup of tea. It was the nicest cup of tea that he had ever tasted. Then she switched the TV on, placed his head on her lap and stroked his hair as he drifted in and out of a drunken haze.

4th February 2020

Now that his exams were over and things were settled in school, Kyle's thoughts turned to other matters. His birthday and Christmas money, and the money that he had earned working for Daryl had depleted. His pocket money didn't last long. When he discussed the matter with his mum, she had told him about the early morning cleaning shifts going in the hospital. Now that he was sixteen and he had his national insurance number, he was eligible to work. The shifts were from five-thirty until eight-thirty. It meant getting up early, but Kyle decided to give it a go. The hospital was a mile across town from Kyle's house and about half a mile from school. He reckoned that if he went to work, he could get changed in the lockers and be in lessons for ten to nine when school started.

To start with, Kyle had had to attend an induction. Luckily it was when he had no mocks. He learned all about the chemicals used for cleaning the hospital, about the NHS trust that he would be working for, and moving and handling things. A lot of it seemed to be a bit pointless, and the whole day had been boring, but at least now he could start working properly.

That first morning, he trudged with his mum across the park to work. There was an uneven path covered in potholes and rather disgusting things like dog muck and litter that ran through the middle. It led to a carpark at the back by the park and the supermarket. A small stream ran through, taking with it toxic remnants of the surrounding rubbish and dubious items left in the park. Even though the landscape was grim, this had been Kyle's childhood playground for as long as he could remember. This was where he wound up and got chased by the older kids, tried his first cigarette, hid when he had played "knock and run" with his friends, built his first den and spent ages constructing rope swings and other items with the various bricks and other materials left long abandoned.

'It gets more dire here every year,' said his mum.

'Yeah, it's not the nicest place, is it? Mum, do you walk here on your own to work every morning?'

'Are you joking? No chance! I go round the road. I like being alive. Anyway, are you ready to do some cleaning?'

Kyle nodded. 'Yeah, I need to start earning some money.'

'You do, and to be honest, I should get a new job now you've nearly finished school.'

'Well, what's so bad about this one?'

'Well, it's been great while you were in school so I could keep an eye on you. But I'm sick of getting up this early every day and the crappy pay. Now I don't need to spy on you all the time seeing as you're behaving.'

Kyle grinned.

'Yeah, I'm sorry, Mum, I told you I wouldn't let you down again. Not after everything you've done for me.'

His mum smiled at him.

'What job do you want to do anyway?' he asked.

'I don't know. I want a change. I might even go and study something new.'

'What like?'

'I don't know, but I'm fed up of cleaning. I need a change. I'd love to train to do something else, like maybe being a teacher.'

Kyle wrinkled his nose up in horror.

'You may laugh, Kyle, but if I can handle you, I reckon I can handle a whole class full of kids.'

'I don't know what I want to do,' said Kyle.

'Well, as long as you don't want to be a delivery boy for a drugs gang or anything else dodgy, I don't think I care what you do, just do something.'

'Yeah, yeah, OK, Mum.'

They reached the hospital. Kyle had only been to the hospital once before and that was to see his nana before she had passed away. It was twenty-past-five and the hospital was quiet. He went through to the cleaning offices and was given his equipment with a set of blue hospital scrubs to wear.

That first morning, Kyle was sent to work with a man called Gary. Gary showed him how to mop the floors of the outpatients' department. Kyle couldn't remember the last time that he had got up this early – he couldn't stop yawning.

'Too early is it for you, mate?' asked Gary.

'Yeah, I'm usually asleep at this time.'

Gary laughed. 'Shock to the system. You'll get used to it, you have to. Any slacking, you'll have Michelle, the supervisor, on your back.'

Gary showed Kyle how to mop the floors. He had to go right back to basics as Kyle had never actually used a mop before. Gary appeared to be able to sense Kyle's embarrassment.

'Don't worry, lad, we've all got to learn.'

Before long, Kyle was mopping away. In a sense, it was therapeutic. The next job was to clean the waiting area of A&E. It was quiet in there with only a couple of people waiting. One man was covered in blood and appeared to be drunk and a lady was sitting at the opposite end of the room, as far away from him as she possibly could. Gary showed Kyle how to clean the chairs and other items while he mopped the floors.

'What you staring at?' slurred the drunk man as Kyle cleaned the chairs by the lady. She looked at Kyle and rolled her eyes.

'Nothing, mate, just doing my job, innit?' said Kyle, taken aback at his rudeness. He felt sure that he was sitting there in A&E because he had probably been rude to someone else who had smacked him one.

'Well, I'm not moving…' he said as he settled himself down, spreading himself across two of the plastic chairs.

Kyle was stumped. Nobody had ever spoken to him like that before. He didn't quite know what to say, or how to react to the drunken man. Gary had told him to clean all of the chairs.

'Oi you, you shut up, leave him do his job or I'll get security to remove you from here and you can go home without being seen, do you understand?' said Gary. 'Ignore him, Kyle, happens all the time in here, he'll go to sleep in a bit hopefully.'

'Yeah, alright, alright…' slurred the man. He simply moved across to the chairs that Kyle had already cleaned. Kyle cleaned the area where he had been. The whole exercise appeared pointless – he felt that he should have just left it as it was.

The next job was to clean the toilets. They were disgusting.

'Get another pair of gloves on, mate,' said Gary.

They put the cleaning signs up around the entrance to the toilets. Kyle walked into the ladies toilets with his double pair of gloves on. The toilet itself wasn't too bad. Gary showed him how to bleach and scrub it with the brush. Then he had to clean the cubicle itself.

'Never move the sanitary bin without checking behind it first,' said Gary as he picked it up. Behind, were what appeared to be used needles. 'That's why we fetch the sharps bin in here.'

Kyle had always assumed that places like hospitals were clean places, places with clinical standards. But this was an eye opener.

'Don't worry, Kyle, you've started off with the worst part of the public areas; we're off to the wards next, they're usually a bit better.'

Kyle and Gary had been asked to finish off in the orthopaedic ward. They made their way up the stairs. As he entered the ward, many of the patients were still asleep and, taking care not to disturb them, he mopped the floor of the ward. It was breakfast time and the trolley had arrived. The nurses pulled the curtains from around the patients.

'Now remember, Kyle, always ask if it's OK to clean around the beds,' said Gary.

Kyle came to an older gentleman lying in a bed.

'Scuse me, sir, am I OK to clean around your bed, please?'

The man didn't reply.

'Sir? Mister?'

The man was sat up, leaning back on his pillows with his eyes open. At first Kyle thought that he was being funny with him. And then he realised that the man's face hadn't moved for some time.

'Er, sir?'

The man's face was grey. His pupils were fixed, his mouth wide open. Kyle began to feel very uneasy as he suspected the worst case scenario – that the man was dead. Kyle had only ever seen one dead person in his life before, his nana after she had passed away. He had remembered her face for months after. It had been awful.

He wasn't quite sure how to make sure that the man was dead; how could he be certain? Unclear and feeling disturbed, he went up to the nurses' station, feeling huge trepidation. If what he suspected was correct, it was terrible!

'Scuse me, nurse, I think that the gentleman in the bed over there is dead.'

'Aw, Mr. Wright? Aw, I'll be over now,' she replied nonchalantly. 'Thanks for letting me know.'

'Well, er, shouldn't I try to, you know, resuscitate him or anything? I learned about it in school last month and in my induction last week, and…'

Realising Kyle's ignorance of the workings of the hospital, the nurse's face straightened.

'No. You're new here, aren't you?'

Kyle nodded.

'Mr. Wright was very ill. He had a "not for resuscitation". That means that if he dies there's no point in trying to resuscitate him, because he's too ill. He had a breathing problem, which means that he can't breathe in proper amounts of air and his lungs were failing.'

'Aw,' said Kyle. 'Didn't know that could happen.'

'Yes.' The nurse nodded. 'Pressing up and down on his chest would probably fracture every bone in his body. Then if he did wake back up, as well as being as ill as he was, he would also be in severe pain from having broken bones that would probably never heal, then he would die a slow, painful death.'

'Aw,' said Kyle. 'Er, it's my first day, sorry.'

'Yes, don't worry, it's OK; we'll sort him out, just need a doctor to confirm death and we'll get him moved.'

'OK,' replied Kyle. 'Well, shall I mop and clean around the bed?'

'Er no, it's OK. We usually move the body first and then give the bed and area a good clean. In the meantime, I'll go and phone his poor family.'

Kyle returned to the bay. He looked over at Mr. Wright. He looked kind, and nice, and peaceful. He felt shocked. He didn't realise that people could just be left to die. But as the nurse explained, it did make sense. If Mr. Wright was that ill, why would they try to bring him back to life? The nurse came to pull the curtain right around the bed so that Mr. Wright was out of view of the rest of the ward. Anyway, it was quarter-to-eight. The time had gone quickly. He had one more ward to do and then he would be finishing.

Shortly after, Michelle, the cleaning supervisor, arrived with her to-do list. Rather abruptly, she came to check up on him as he mopped the floor.

'Oi, you've used the same bucket for the whole floor! That won't do, you need to change it half way across. Go back and do it again.'

'Oh, OK,' replied Kyle, feeling demoralised.

His arms were beginning to ache slightly from all the mopping and scrubbing that he had been doing. Although he usually did his bench presses and press-ups as part of his fitness regime for football, he seemed to be using muscles that he never usually would and his arms ached as he went into the sluice and filled the bucket up with water and bleach like Gary had shown him to do. Once he had finished the floor, seats and surfaces it was nearly eight-thirty.

'Very well done, Kyle, you've done a thorough job here,' said Michelle as she scrubbed the surfaces in the next bay. Despite her brash demeanour, Michelle was obviously the kind of person who liked things to be done properly. As she got stuck into the job, Kyle beamed with pride.

'So, Kyle, did you enjoy it then? Or have we broken you and you're not coming back?' asked Michelle as she booked his cleaning trolley back into the cleaning department.

'Yeah, it was OK, I think I can do it if you want me to come back? The man dead in the bed freaked me a bit though.'

Michelle's face dropped.

'Yeah, it's not nice, but it does happen. It's just unfortunate that it was on your first day, mate. Hopefully you won't see anything like that again for a while.'

'I don't know, I thought when you died, someone tried to resuscitate you, but the nurse said to leave him. I didn't know that happened…'

'We've all got to go sometime, mate, this was his time.'

'Aw,' said Kyle. He still couldn't quite get his head around the whole thing. The more that he thought about it, the more it freaked him out.

'So will we be seeing you back in two days?' she asked.

Kyle nodded. 'Yeah.'

'Well, I'm always looking for cleaners. Don't forget I've got shifts at the weekend as well, slightly better pay. I know you're limited in your hours because of your age, but we can work something out…'

'Yeah, thanks. It's my last year of exams, but if I get some spare time I'll certainly consider it.'

Kyle headed down to the staffroom and the locker where he had put his things. He felt dirty. He had already had a shower when he had woken up, but now he felt as if he needed another one. There was a shower in the men's toilet. Next time he came to work, he would bring his change of clothes and have a quick shower before walking to school.

Kyle got dressed and headed over to school, munching the cereal bar that his mum had packed for him and drinking a flask of tea. He felt more awake at this time of the morning after doing a cleaning shift than he had ever felt in his life. He had a rim around his head where the hairnet had cut into his skin and no matter how hard he blew it, there was a faint smell of bleach mixed with unwashed body fluids inside his nose.

It was nearly quarter to nine and school was just around the corner. Yet Kyle felt as if he had done a whole day's work in just under three hours.

Try as he might, Kyle could not get the vision of Mr. Wright's dead body out of his mind. As he walked, he reflected on the last three hours. The more that he thought about it, the more he wondered about Mr. Wright; what was he like? Where did he live? What was his family like? What was his life like? What did he used to do? Was he a good person? Something else spooked him, that the man was older, like Grandad. Things like that made Kyle realise that Grandad was getting old. If anything ever happened to him, what would Kyle do without him? Cold shudders began to travel up his spine at the very thought and he began to feel tearful. Maybe this job was going to be much harder than he had first thought.

Kyle was almost looking forward to going to class and learning the rest of his GCSE curriculum. Sitting in class just having to listen would be easy compared to what he had just seen. At least it would stop him having to think about Mr. Wright and worry about Grandad becoming old and dying.

9th March 2020

Kyle had been working in the hospital for the past three weeks. Getting up early and going to school was manageable but tiring. For some reason, even though he felt so tired, after working in the hospital all morning, the work that he had to do in school seemed easy in comparison. He revised in the library at break times with his friends, went home and did his coursework, then, unless he was going out to play football with his friends or going to the gym, he stayed in. At the weekends, he hung out with his friends. And if there was a match on he went with Grandad to watch Wrexham play. Now that he was up to date with his school work, things weren't too bad. Plus, getting up early stopped him from spending long periods of time on his computer and phone. When he needed to get up for work, he went to bed at nine o'clock. He had a newfound respect for his mum who did eight hour shifts in the hospital.

Kyle had never really cleaned anywhere except for his room before he had started working in the hospital. In a couple of weeks, he had learned the ropes and things like how to mop, scrub and wipe. However, just as he had got used to the job, things began to change.

There was all this talk of "coronavirus". It was a virus that caused people to have great difficulty in breathing. It seemed to involve a cough and temperature, a bit like the flu apparently. They said that it had come from China.

'Just sounds like another version of the flu to me,' said Gary. 'I dunno what all the fuss is about.'

But the hospital was taking things seriously. Things were changing at an alarming rate. The cleaners had been asked to attend a meeting one Monday evening to discuss their roles. They had also been asked to have a training session on the new methods of cleaning the hospital that would be coming in should the hospital be affected by coronavirus. Kyle sighed when he found out about it; his first induction, although necessary, had been boring.

'God, I could do without this tonight,' said his mum, complaining as they walked over to the meeting. 'I've only just come home from there, and now I've got to go back; this better be important.'

Some of the other cleaners that Kyle knew were there. Michelle appeared with a couple of other people who were high up in the trust. One of them, a really posh-sounding man who was some kind of doctor began to talk. He spoke about coronavirus, how deadly it was in other places and how it was making its way here. There were no cases confirmed in North Wales as yet, but everyone felt that it was coming. Apparently it took a week for symptoms to show. There were patients in London and other big cities who had caught it who were on ventilators. From now on, when cleaning dangerous areas where there could be confirmed cases, everyone had to wear protective equipment. This included masks, gloves, aprons, and if cleaning in areas with confirmed coronavirus, hazmats. Kyle didn't really understand what they were talking about. He just sat and nodded. Cleaning certain high risk areas such as intensive care and the high dependency unit would entail wearing the equipment.

'It'll be like that SARS,' said Gary. 'All this fuss, and it'll be over before it's begun.'

'This is just great,' said his mum as they walked back home. 'The job is hard enough, now we've got to do a load of new things, and what's more it's going to be dangerous to do them.'

'What? The virus?'

'I'm sick of that place. I'm thinking of getting another job anyway. If it gets much worse, I'll be leaving sooner than later. I should start looking for a different job; I'm sick of cleaning toilets as it is.'

'Yeah, Mum, you can get a different job to that. There's loads of jobs out there. What would you want to do?'

'Dunno, I'm going to have a good think and have a look around. I'm not wearing bloody suits to clean in with a mask though, it's hot enough in there as it is - a shop, I'd like to work in a clothes shop. I'd get the same wage for probably less hassle.'

'Yeah? Well why don't you have a look round in town? I'm sure there's loads of jobs going.'

'Yeah, there are always places advertising. I'll have a look next week.'

13th March 2020

'Well, I dunno what all the bloody fuss is about, it sounds like the bloody flu to me,' said Grandad.

Unlike Grandad, people in Kyle's work were feeling uneasy about things. The hospital was already trying to order more protective equipment and changing procedures. The volunteers' shop and café had been shut until further notice.

It wasn't just in the hospital; it was starting to impact the rest of the world too. All week, shops and other businesses had started to shut down. Today after school, Kyle had an appointment at the barber's. It was the last day that it was going to be open according to Katie the manageress and then they were shutting until further notice.

Kyle had read a bit about it. From the basic knowledge of biology that he had, from what he understood it was a virus that got into your body cells and took them over to replicate. It was passed on by air-borne droplets. Kyle wasn't sure what to think, but one thing was for certain, if they were worried and taking it seriously in the hospital, he felt inclined to be worried too. He had been told that the outpatients' department would be shutting with all clinics planned to be cancelled and they would be concentrating more on A&E with the bigger focus on deep cleaning. Even visitors would soon be banned.

After the meeting, a training session was arranged for the cleaners. It was a day of going through the new cleaning procedures, what chemicals had to be used, how things needed to be cleaned and procedures about hazardous waste transfer. It was to be held the week after next.

'Well, Kyle, this is the first school day that you've ever skived off that I've given you a note for before you've done it,' said his mum. Kyle grinned at her. He was that on top of his work that he was confident that he could catch up.

Then another bad thing had happened, football had been cancelled. Not just his five-aside, but all the Premier League games! Kyle loved football… he was gutted. What would he do if he couldn't go with his Grandad and watch his beloved Wrexham play?

Everyone in school thought that it was just a passing phase.

'Aw, it'll all blow over in a couple of weeks.'

'Yeah, we'll be OK. I can't believe the cinema's shut!'

The next week, there was an announcement from the government. All schools were to shut down with immediate effect from 20th March. Everyone had to be home-schooled unless you were the child of a keyworker and it wasn't feasible to stay at home. Everywhere that was fun to be was shutting down; the cinema, the bowling alley, the sports centre, shops selling non-essential items, pubs and restaurants.

They said that people needed to stay in the house and could only go out for exercise purposes or to buy essential items. Everyone aged over seventy and people with certain underlying health conditions would need to shield. That meant that they couldn't leave the house. Grandad was over seventy. Kyle was aware that as he was working in such a dangerous environment, he would be putting Grandad at risk if he went anywhere near him. Although Grandad was usually fit and well, they had said in the induction that older people, especially men, were at high risk.

Kyle realised that Grandad would be very unlikely to put up with restrictions being placed on him. Grandad wasn't scared of anything or anyone. Kyle mulled it over with a sense of foreboding; not seeing his grandad would be the worst thing of all.

'They've shut Shone's café, and now the bloody football? They're saying don't go to the shop unless you have to, what the bloody hell is going on?' Grandad said.

'I don't know, but it sounds bad, Grandad.'

'Bullcrap. I'm not being told what to do, sitting in the bloody house all day. I'll drive myself mad.'

School was to be closed for the foreseeable future. As he mopped away, Kyle wondered what to do. If things were shutting down and he couldn't go anywhere or do anything, he needed to think about what he could do. He had just been paid his first wages. If the virus was that serious and he wouldn't be able to buy anything, what did he need?

He had planned to buy himself a new pair of football boots when he got his money, but it looked as if football was going to be cancelled for a good few weeks. Kyle was proud of his physique; the last thing that he wanted to do was put weight on from not exercising. After school, he planned to go into town to the sports shop and buy himself a pair of new trainers. The regular pair that he had for everyday wear hurt his tendons when he tried to exercise in them. Last week he had been to the opticians because his old glasses that he sometimes wore for schoolwork or when he was tired felt weird. They said that his sight test had actually improved from last time that he had had it checked last year and changed his prescription. Kyle wondered if it was because he was getting a lot more sleep? And not spending so much time on computer games and his phone. He had seen a new pair of smart glasses that he liked and wouldn't usually be able to afford. If things were shutting down, he should buy them now that he had the money to save having a free uncool pair.

When he thought about what pair of new trainers to buy, Kyle remembered that he did have trainers that would do, but he never wanted to wear them ever again. They were the ones that he had bought when he had started working for Daryl. He had condemned them to the back of the cupboard since the day that he had left the gang and tried to forget all about them. They belonged to the part of his life that he wanted to forget about. He shuddered as he remembered back to how desperately he had wanted those trainers. He had forgotten about them until now. When he remembered back, he hated the thought of them even being in his house. They were the most expensive item that he had ever bought – they had nearly cost him his life. Kyle decided that no matter how desperate he was for new trainers, he would never wear them again. They needed to go.

Back at home after school, he opened the cupboard under the stairs – there they were, right at the back, the luminous stripes reflecting the light from the hallway. His hands trembled as he pulled them out. Sense told him that he should wear them, it was almost wasteful not to. But his heart lurched with disgust as he saw them for the first time in nearly five months. Maybe he could sell them? But what if they brought him bad luck for profiting from his ill-gotten gains? No. He shuddered as he remembered back to the last night that he had worn them.

Kyle needed to get rid of them, not just in the bin, but to destroy them for good. Now that he had taken them out, he couldn't bring himself to put them back in the cupboard. Shuddering as he touched them, he placed them in a carrier bag and walked down the road into town. As he looked down at the bag that he was carrying, he contemplated what to do. Maybe he could throw them in a rubbish bin? No, not final enough. A filthy pool in the park where they would rot away? No, not quick enough. Maybe he could take them to work tomorrow, and throw them in the hospital incinerator. Then they would be gone forever. But while he thought about what to do with them, he decided to go and try and talk some sense into Grandad about coronavirus.

'Alright, son?'

'Yeah, not bad, Grandad.'

'Where you off to?'

'Er, just to get rid of these,' replied Kyle, holding up the bag.

'What are they?'

'Well, it's stupid really… it's the trainers, the first thing I bought with my money off Daryl. I just don't want them. I want rid of them, they're a bad omen.'

Grandad smiled at him.

'Come with me, son,' he said.

'No, Grandad, I can't come in…'

'We're not going in. And yes, you can, I don't give a bloody toss about this stupid crap about a virus.'

Grandad had a fire going in his incinerator in the back garden; he was burning the remnants of the last season in preparation for the new one. Perfect.

'In there?' He indicated to the incinerator.

Kyle smiled to himself as he tipped the trainers out of his bag and placed them on top of the other rubbish. He watched them burn; it was cathartic, watching them melt away, just like it had felt watching the fire engulf his phone in Jade's house.

'Better now, lad?'

'Yeah.'

'I'll get us a brew, come in.'

'Grandad, I can't come in, we've got to start being careful. I'm telling you, it's dangerous.'

'Well,' said Grandad indignantly. 'OK, we'll sit outside if you insist, but I don't bloody care. It's a load of old fuss about nothing.'

'I'm telling you, Grandad, it's bad, and it's coming round here. We all need to start being careful.'

Kyle and his grandad sipped their tea and sat in the sun as the aroma of burned plastic filled the air. He felt as if a great weight had been taken off his shoulders, as if the final material connection that he had to Daryl and his gang had been eliminated, gone. Kyle felt relieved. But he also felt sad, sad for an entirely different reason.

'I'm going to have to stop coming round here like this soon, Grandad, just until the virus is over.'

Grandad stopped drinking his tea in mid-sip.

'Why?'

'Well, you know, because of the virus. It's dangerous. You're supposed to be shielding because you're at risk.'

'Me? Bloody shielding? They can have that. I'm not bloody shielding! I'm not having someone in an office in London telling me what to do.'

Much as Kyle tried his best to persuade his grandad about how bad the new threat of the virus was, Grandad was having none of it. He told Kyle that he was still going to the shop and that he was not shielding. Grandad's defiance made Kyle's blood run cold. Kyle felt sure that from what had been discussed in the hospital, sooner or later he would have some horror stories to tell. What if the story was about Grandad? Kyle didn't want that; he just wished that his grandad would listen to sense.

Kyle and Grandad eventually had to agree to disagree about the virus. After he left Grandad's, Kyle walked into town to see if there were any trainers that he could buy with the money that he had left. Town was unusually quiet. There was no dodging people as you walked down the pedestrianised high street. There was nobody standing chatting. A few of the shops had already closed down. The coffee shops and cafes were empty. There was a sense that an apocalypse was coming, and nobody could predict what it was. Not an obvious apocalypse, like an asteroid, or a nuclear war, but something far worse, a silent assassin, something almost superhuman. Kyle didn't like it; it felt creepy.

He walked into the sports shop. There was a sale on. He tried on a few pairs of trainers and decided on a smart pair of Nikes. Buying them he felt proud, honest, good – he had worked hard for them and they were all his.

Next, he went to the opticians and bought the glasses that he had liked.

As he walked back home past the bowling alley, he saw that the doors were shut and the lights were off. There was a note on the door advising that it was shut until further notice. No way! This could not be happening. How on earth could his life be heading this way? Everything was being taken from him – his freedom, his life, everything! It was all just so unfair! Apart from his daily exercise, there was only one place that Kyle could now go and have a real excuse to leave the house – he was now a "keyworker".

His mum was there when he got home. 'Well, I went to town when I finished work today and asked in a few shops about getting another job,' she said. 'They all said they don't know what's happening with the virus so they're not taking anyone on - so it looks like I'm stuck scrubbing toilets for now.'

23rd March 2020

It was official, the UK was now in lockdown.

It had been coming for a couple of weeks. Nobody knew how long it was going to be for. Everyone was under the impression that it would be only be for a few weeks. Yet Italy had been locked down for a while now, and cases of the virus were reported to be still rampant there. Kyle found it difficult to fathom that just a few weeks ago he was in school with his friends, planning what they were going to do in the summer after their exams. Now, he wasn't even allowed to see any of them! Not even outside.

Kyle and his mum had to go to another meeting at work. Some members of staff who had underlying health conditions and the few that were older than seventy had been ordered to start shielding. This meant that the cleaning department was now short-staffed and there were other additional hours going in the daytime and weekend. He had been asked to work his usual shift every morning from Monday to Friday instead of three days a week together with some extra hours. Due to his age, Kyle was not able to work for more than a certain number of hours each day. But tempted as he was by the extra money, he decided to stick to mornings. He had worked so hard in school to get up to speed with everything that to prioritise his job made no sense. If he did mornings, he realised that he could spend the rest of his day doing his work. If he felt able to, he would then put his name down for more shifts in the future. But hopefully, this would not last that long.

His mum was angry.

'It's not fair. I'm busting a gut, we're putting ourselves at risk every day, and what for? So other people can sit on their arses all day on bloody furlough? We earn bog all! And what for? So we can pull everyone else out of the shit?'

'I know, Mum.'

'Kyle, why don't you just give it up for a bit 'til things settle down?'

'No, I'm OK, Mum. Anyway, I live with you. If you get it, I'll probably get it.'

'Aww, don't say that. It's all making me anxious just thinking about it.'

'Anyway, I don't think I can stay in, it drives me nuts.'

'Yeah, and what are we going to get from the NHS as a thanks? Probably privatised by that crap government who don't give a toss about the likes of us. They haven't even given us enough protective equipment.'

'I know.'

'Only for ITU and areas of concern. They haven't even got any tests to see who's got it! Any Tom, Dick or Harry could have it, so why aren't we being protected from them? They've put us in a catch twenty-two!'

Kyle's mum was mad. And rightly so. There was limited protective equipment in the hospital and this was being saved for certain high risk procedures. But it made no sense at all that everyone was being told to shield, yet in the hospital, staff were being told that they didn't need protective equipment unless they were engaging in high risk procedures. Furthermore, there was still no established testing system in place for patients who were suspected of having COVID-19.

The next day in work, Kyle scrubbed away. He winced every time someone coughed, or sneezed, or looked unwell. As most people in hospital looked unwell, he walked around feeling constantly paranoid.

Michelle had asked Kyle if he would clean the intensive care department. When he entered ITU he was given protective equipment to clean with. He wanted to keep it on for the whole shift, but was told that he would need to remove it when he left the area. This made no sense to him at all. If COVID was in intensive care, it would have had to get there; the patient would have been in an ambulance, in A&E, in the hospital. Yet they were now segregating areas where patients and staff had to be kept apart. It was madness!

This week was the first week of working from home. After he finished work, Kyle had a shower, went home and logged onto his computer. Diligent in his approach, he started off with great gusto. Under the new government regulations, you were allowed to do one hour of exercise a day. Kyle decided that just before lunch time he would go for a run to break his day up. Certainly, after a morning of doing maths and history, he needed to clear his head. Not the only frustrated pupil, his phone began to ping.

'Bored.com.'

'This is shit.'

'Yep! Fed up already.'

Roxanne had set up a group messenger chat. As they weren't allowed to see each other, they could only keep in touch that way.

'Sod off, already been to work for 3 hours u lightweights scrubbing bogs.'

'I wish I could get out of the house and scrub bogs.'

'This crap sucks.'

'Anyone fancy meeting up in the field halfway up the mountain where no one can see us?'

'I'm up for it.'

'Me too, see you up there.'

'I'm coming.'

'Yes, sounds good, I need to get out.'

The government said you weren't allowed to meet up with other people, even outside. There was no way that his friends were going to stay in and adhere to the rules.

'I'll meet you on my hour of exercise. Staying 2m away from you all though, just cleaned a ward full of ill people who could have COVID.'

'Urgh, don't worry, not coming anywhere near you.'

Kyle knew that he really shouldn't be meeting up with his friends outside, but he could not stand the thought of staying in. Surely if he kept two metres away it would be OK, wouldn't it?'

He changed into a pair of shorts. Then he went for a run towards the mountain range just outside town. He had arranged to meet Mo and Roxanne halfway up in the field behind a layby where they sometimes went to hang out. It was Mo that had told him about it; it was off the beaten track. As he ran, the clean air filled his lungs and he felt immediately better. After a couple of miles, he reached the meeting place. He stopped to catch his breath and looked down over the town. He could see the hospital, and the area where the park was. Spring was unfolding. The world looked lovely, but the story that the unfolding nature told was all a façade. Something else far more deadly was unfolding in the world. Yet in the fields up the mountains, the birds sang, the rabbits ran around, the squirrels scampered up and down trees. But the humans? The humans were nowhere to be seen.

Kyle crept into the undergrowth and just behind the hedge, out of the way of anyone else who might walk up the mountain. He walked across the field towards the old tin shed in the middle where Mo had told him to go to.

First up the hill was Mo on his bike. He shoved his bike over the hedge and walked across the field to join Kyle.

'Good idea, to do something. I need a break from studying.'

'Mate, I haven't got time to be bored. I've been in work all morning. That hospital's getting crazy, man.'

'Hi guys,' said Roxanne as she came up the hill, puffing like a tractor. 'God, I'm unfit.' She hopped over the boundary shrubbery and made her way to join them.

They sat for a good hour, just chatting, messing around, and putting the world to rights before it started to drizzle. His friends sat next to each other seemed to have no knowledge of the virus or how dangerous it was. Kyle explained that they all had to keep two metres apart and why. Nobody seemed to be taking him seriously.

'Mate, I feel like a leper with you sitting that far away.'

'Na, trust me, this shit sounds dangerous.'

'Na, it's all a conspiracy.'

'I don't think it is, not from what I've seen in the hospital.'

'Ain't no way I can do home-schooling for long. It just feels wrong doing work like that at home; home is where you're meant to be able to chill.'

'Yeah, well, hopefully, it'll only be for a couple of weeks.'

'I dunno, we're a couple of weeks behind Italy. It's getting worse there, not better.'

'But they've been locked down for about two weeks. Surely if that's the case nobody can pass it around?'

'Dunno, it's pretty bad there though.'

Gradually, they all stopped talking about the virus. They talked about things that they had done over the last week, about gossip from school. They had fun, and felt normal again, if only for a short time.

'Well, better get back. My mum's on my case, making me do the four hours a day like they say we should be,' said Roxanne.

'Na, mine has no idea what we're meant to be doing,' said Mo. 'Losing motivation.'

'Well,' said Roxanne, 'we should download Zoom, then we can get together for a maths session.'

'OK, let's do a zoom and go over it,' said Kyle.

Feeling grateful to be out and to have managed to see his friends, Kyle ran back down the hill and home with a spring in his step. Surely things couldn't go on longer than a couple of weeks, could they?

2nd April 2020

The hospital had confirmed cases of coronavirus. Kyle was feeling petrified, his mum even more so. The protective equipment that had been promised had still not arrived.

'I've gone off with stress for a couple of weeks, there's no way I'm doing that job without protection. I'm not working there with nothing to stop me getting it, and I don't think you should.'

'They say it's on the way, Mum, and I wear it in ITU, where I seem to be put most of the time now.'

'Yeah, because you're young and fit, and apparently unlikely to die from it if you catch it.'

'Well, if it's in the hospital, that means it's got to be everywhere else too.'

'Balls to it. I'll get drunk in the garden like people on furlough on their eighty percent pay seem to be doing. I don't give a shit about being an NHS hero, or people clapping for me, I'm not dying working for peanuts, and I don't think you should either.'

'Mum, I'd go mad if I couldn't go to work.'

Life as they knew it had changed beyond all recognition. Staff had now been told that they were supposed to be wearing protective equipment all the time, yet there was still a national shortage. Then they were told that protective equipment wasn't to be worn unless patients were confirmed as having COVID yet still, nearly two weeks later, there was still no proper testing system in place: the whole situation was beyond ridiculous. Staff were getting the distinct impression that they were being blatantly lied to.

Kyle carried on going to work while the rest of the world stood still. The people that he knew who worked seemed to be off work on furlough where they got eighty percent pay for doing absolutely nothing. It seemed that life on earth had taken an odd dichotomy; there were those who carried on in ignorant bliss, and those who were working in the thick of things and were facing the threat of COVID-19 on a daily basis. There wasn't much in between.

As dangerous as his job was, Kyle felt glad that he had a reason to get out of the house and do something, even if it was cleaning in a dangerous environment. It was hard enough to sit down for a long period of time and do his schoolwork after he had finished work. But no matter how much he scrubbed himself in the hospital shower afterwards, he constantly felt unclean, contaminated, as if there was an invisible entity poisoning his very soul. Every time he coughed, or sneezed, as he often did in the spring pollen, he began to worry.

In work, Michelle had asked him to work in the high risk areas on a permanent basis. He wore protective equipment for his shifts. For most of the time, he cleaned the intensive care and high dependency units. Hospital policy advised cleaning high risk areas more frequently. Being sixteen, Kyle was not supposed to be doing unsociable hours or dangerous jobs. But as his mum suspected, Michelle advised him that he had been asked to clean the high risk areas during his morning shift because he was young, fit and unlikely to get the virus. Other staff refused. Kyle had figured that he would rather clean high risk areas in protective equipment than low risk areas in none. By now some of the staff who had carried on working and had no underlying medical conditions, like his mum, had been signed off work with stress and anxiety. Outpatient clinics had been cancelled, A&E was quiet and visiting patients had been stopped. Therefore, the hospital was much quieter than usual.

'This is just nuts; how the hell can they expect me to tell you lot to clean areas when you've got nothing to do it in?' complained Michelle. 'It's not fair, and I'm getting all the bloody flack.'

The hospital was trying to recruit more staff and work was becoming harder. There was a horrible air of uncertainty and trepidation. More and more restrictions were being put in place; the hospital had gone from a place that was alive and vibrant, full of hope where people came to be made better, to a place where nobody wanted to be: a desolate and barren entity, like a nuclear power plant just about to be decommissioned running on a skeleton of staff. But the truth was, everyone was working hard behind the scenes. Staff had been deployed. Intensive care was full, as were the outlying wards. Two members of staff had already died of COVID-19. Even though Kyle didn't know who they were, it made it seem all the more real somehow.

Kyle's main concern remained his grandad. Grandad had refused to adhere to the suggestion that he should be shielding and continued about his business as if nothing was happening. As he sat studying, Kyle's phone buzzed. Grandad's number flashed up.

'Eh, mate, you'll never guess what, Ned from down the road has got it. He's in ITU.'

'No way, Grandad! That's bad.'

'I know, with his chest and his heart, he's not a well bloke anyway.'

'Yeah, well, maybe now you'll realise how bad it is, Grandad.'

The next day in work, Kyle entered ITU in his hazmat. He could just about make out Ned covered in tubes.

Kyle had seen unwell people before. He had seen people who had passed away, he had cleaned around bodies as they had been waiting to be transported to the morgue. But he had never seen anyone that he knew who was so unwell before. The man lying in the bed did not look like Ned, and, as much as he tried to stop himself, Kyle could not stop putting Grandad's face where Ned's was.

Why, oh why, would Grandad not listen to him about how dangerous this thing was? All Grandad saw was someone trying to deprive him of his liberties. Yet this thing was real. COVID did not care how loved someone was, whether they were a good person, their actions or their attitude – this thing was coming for anyone. As soon as he finished work, Kyle phoned Grandad. He just had to talk to him, to know he was OK.

'How are you, Grandad?'

'I'm fine, son. Apparently it doesn't look too good for Ned though. They can't go and visit him so they can't see him, but Rita and the family have been told to expect the worst.'

'Yeah, I know. And going out, not being careful, that could have just as well been you. Maybe now you'll start being a bit more careful?'

'Well, how can he have got it? They say he's only been down the road to get a paper.'

'Yeah, to the shop, where everyone else has been standing, breathing, touching things. Of course he'll get it.'

'Well, bloody hell.'

'I'm telling you, Grandad, you need to be more careful. Why do you think when I drop you things off I wipe them down? And why I won't come into the house? I've been cleaning the ITU where people like Ned have been lying.'

'Yeah, but you're not ill though, are you?'

'I might have it and not know, Grandad. I could just be carrying it for up to a week they reckon, and nobody would be any the wiser.'

The penny still didn't seemed to be dropping where Grandad was concerned. No matter how hard Kyle attempted to convince him, his attempts were futile.

Kyle and his friends had continued to meet up outside every few days. Kyle knew that it was wrong and he felt guilty, but he couldn't stand not seeing anyone. After work, and after going home and doing his schoolwork, he craved to feel normal, human, even if it was just for a short amount of time. When he met his friends, even though Kyle was always careful to physically stay away from people, his friends initially hadn't been. Now, everyone sat or stood two metres apart. They were always moaning about posts that other people were putting up, and how sad and pathetic they were. By now, everyone knew someone who had it or had died because of COVID. Most people had come to realise that the virus was deadly. Other people, especially younger people, weren't being so careful. Apparently there were areas of the estate where people were just carrying on as if nothing was happening.

'Oh my god,' said Roxanne. 'Leanne is so pathetic. Lucy's grandma has just died of it, and apparently there she was putting posts about COVID being a lie, and her hair being a mess and not being able to get her nails done.'

'You're joking.'

'No. Not like she wouldn't have known, seeing as she lives next door to her.'

Kyle was glad that he was no longer active on social media; after what he saw in the hospital every day he felt sure that he would become angry about other people's ignorance. Other people like Roxanne had found ways forwards. She had started painting watercolours and selling them on Etsy. Mo had joined an agency and was planning to do some evening shifts in a frozen food factory. The hospital had managed to recruit some more cleaning staff who were waiting for a start date. Work was harder. But the situation was worse in other places.

'Kyle, we need cleaners at the other hospital down the coast,' said Michelle. 'They're dropping like flies there and finding it hard to recruit. They've asked me if I can spare anyone. Apparently they'll pay you a bit more than here and put you up in accommodation.'

'Seriously, Michelle? I'm sixteen, I'm studying for my exams, besides, how on earth would I get there?'

'Well, I just thought I'd ask in case you want a change of scene. I've got more starting soon so it won't be for a few weeks, but I've been asked to ask everyone.'

'Why would I want to do that?' said Kyle, looking at Michelle in disbelief.

'Between you and me, I don't want to lose you, Kyle, but I've been asked to ask you, so there, I've asked the question.'

Even the offer of more money wasn't tempting. There was nothing to spend it on. Kyle had ordered himself another pair of trainers and some new clothes, but there was nowhere to go to wear them to look cool.

Being on his own a lot meant that Kyle had time to think. Everything was so odd, and when Kyle reflected on it all he couldn't believe how much had changed. This time last year, he thought that people who had smart cars, money and cool clothes from selling drugs were boss! Now he knew that that this was not the case.

Daryl was a constant presence at the back of Kyle's mind. What had happened to him? Where had he ended up? Despite the fact that he hadn't seen him for so long, he still had an inherent fear that one day he would bump into him. He had heard nothing from him or about him since he had seen Jason before Christmas. After he had made it clear that he would not divulge any information about his part in the gang, Kyle had had no further contact from the police, so there was no way that he could be accused of being a grass. Surely, if he ever did bump into Daryl again he would have no gripe with Kyle? Would he? Unless he suspected that it was he, Kyle, who had started the fire?

After he finished his shift, Kyle walked back home from work through the park. As he approached the entrance, he skirted around a car parked in the middle of the pavement. As he walked past, the driver's window dropped and Kyle heard a familiar voice.

'Alright, Kyle.'

Daryl!

Kyle's heart stopped as an impending sense of doom washed over him. His heart leapt up into his throat and then dived back down into his trainers. He had dreaded this moment for months. Slowly he turned around.

'Long time, no see.'

Daryl looked different; weathered, greyer, his hair not cut in the usual style which seemed to disguise the fact that he was balding. He had lost weight. The car that he was driving was a wreck and it looked as desperate as he did. The very sight of him sent beads of sweat dripping from Kyle's forehead..

'Daryl.'

'Yeah I'm back, thought we'd move operations back up this way. I've been trying to get in touch with you, Kyle…' he said, the pregnant pause filled with accusation.

'Yeah… my phone burned in the fire, remember? I saw you at the shop just before I went back for it?' replied Kyle, trying to sound as clear and eloquent as he could, hoping to establish his alibi. But at the mention of "the fire", Kyle felt his face begin to burn up as his heart pumped harder. He shifted around uncomfortably and looked at his feet, unable to meet Daryl's piercing green eyes for more than a few seconds.

'Of course, of course… well, anyway, I was hoping that I'd bump into you. We're looking for workers to do deliveries again. How do you fancy a business opportunity?'

Daryl spoke to Kyle in the same manner as he had before, with an uncomfortable underlying tone of malice. He was not asking Kyle to start working for him, he was telling him to.

Doing deliveries again!

Since Kyle had last seen Daryl, his life had turned around. He had knuckled down, stayed out of trouble, sat all of his mock exams, got a job! He had a life now! His mum and grandad were finally proud of him - he was no longer anybody's slave. Much as he didn't like the idea of angering Daryl, there was no way that Kyle was going back to that world, not ever! He shook his head. There was no point in pretending.

'I'm not interested, Daryl.'

Daryl's face hardened.

'It's a business opportunity, Kyle.'

'Like I said, I'm not interested.'

'Kyle.' Daryl glared at him. 'Remember, you're still in the gang… you can't just leave, you're one of us now. Now come round to this address at four o'clock today and I'll...'

'No, not anymore,' replied Kyle. 'I've moved on. I don't owe the gang nothing.'

'Kyle, you will come…'

'No chance. Like I said, I owe you nothing, man. I'm done.'

With that, he walked off. Daryl drove slowly along next to him for a few metres until the road ran out.

'Kyle, I ain't going away that easily... if I say you're working for us, you're working for us, now get in the car.'

Kyle stopped, turned around and looked Daryl straight in the eye. If he kept away from Daryl, he wouldn't be able to engage with him. Eventually, he would have to leave him alone wouldn't he?

'No, man, I'm done, like I said, I don't owe you or your gang nothing. Not a "Bic" like me, as you call us.'

Daryl's eyes narrowed.

'I gave you your package back, Daryl, the one that apparently you were going to get someone to do me over for, so I'd feel obliged to stay? You tried to screw me over, then get rid of me; how do you do it, in the boot of the car, in the quarry?'

Daryl stared long and hard at Kyle. Eventually he spoke.

'Who's been talking, Kyle?'

'No one.'

'Jason. He's on borrowed time as it is, Kyle.'

'What do you mean? I… I haven't seen Jason. Anyway, I'm not interested.'

Kyle turned and walked off up the path.

'I know where you live, Kyle, and I'll be round.'

Kyle stopped walking. Daryl was a real life crook who was wanted by real life police. It should have been simple – he should have been arrested, but he hadn't been. Unlike the adventure films that Kyle had watched, unlike the books that his mum had read to him when he was little, the good guys didn't always win, did they? Kids like him, Kyle, kids who were disposable, and expendable, stood little chance against villains like Daryl in real life. There was no chance of changing into Spiderman or the Hulk. None of his mates were going to morph into a member of the A-team and pull up in an armoured van with blacked-out windows: this was just Kyle and Daryl.

'Maybe you do, Daryl, but I don't care. I still ain't working for you.'

'You will, Kyle, you just need a bit of time.'

'No chance.'

'You'll be very sorry.'

'Never, mate. Anyway, you'd better keep your head down, man, don't you know the police are looking for you?'

Daryl's face dropped at the mention of the police; his eyes narrowed in suspicion.

'You'd better tell me who's been talking, Kyle.'

'Be lucky, man.'

Kyle walked off swiftly through the park. At least Daryl couldn't follow him in there in his car. Praying that he wasn't going to jump out and stick a knife in his back, Kyle kept walking. Shortly after, he heard Daryl's car wheel-spin off. All Kyle could do was pray that by the time that he got home, Daryl would not be waiting outside for him with a knife. Regardless, something told him that it wasn't the last that he was going to see of Daryl.

20th April 2020

To his relief, Kyle had not seen or heard from Daryl again.

Lockdown had gone on for over a month now, and each day the hospital was seeing more and more cases of COVID-19.

Now they had proper protective equipment. Staff were to wear the equipment regardless of whether patients were suspected of having COVID-19 or not. Kyle's mum had returned to work, accepting that she could do her job in the correct equipment.

The situation was starting to get to people who had to stay in. Initially, people seemed to have sat in their gardens enjoying the sunny weather and having a ball. But now, everyone was becoming miserable and bored. It was as if everything that made people happy, things to look forward to and things that made life worth living, no longer existed. Everyone had presumed that it would only all be for a couple of weeks – it wasn't. There was no prospect of lockdown ending anytime soon and cases of COVID were rising. Kyle was sick of it already. He felt somehow cheated, not just out of his social life, or school, but out of all the hard work that he had been doing in the hospital.

'Payday this week,' said his mum with a smile.

'Great,' replied Kyle, his face expressionless.

'Why the long face?'

'Well, it's not like I can use it to go out. Or buy smart clothes that everyone is going to see, or spend it on having fun, is it?'

'I know, it's not much fun for us, is it? That snotty cow down the road at number ten walks in the house every time she sees me coming up the road. As if I'm covered in disease because I've been to work. I feel like chucking my dirty laundry in her garden. I bet if she was ill, she'd expect the ward she was on to be cleaned! As long as I've known her, she's never even had a job.'

All his friends were miserable; it was as if they were losing everything, mainly their freedom which everyone was beginning to resent. But unlike his friends who were not in the position of being able to see the harsh reality of COVID, the more Kyle saw of the hospital, the more he understood. The ward structures were changing on a daily basis. Only the most unwell of patients went to hospital. Everybody else stayed as far as they could away from the place. There were now separate areas of COVID positive and COVID negative patients. Due to the aerosol generating procedures, Kyle got to wear a full hazmat and mask. Even though it was hot inside, he felt protected.

There were more and more odd symptoms being associated with COVID in addition to fever, cough and loss of taste and smell; headaches, stomach upsets, diarrhoea, throat constriction. Rightfully so, everybody in the hospital was assuming that everyone and anyone who was unwell could have coronavirus. Kyle mulled it all over as he scrubbed the floor.

Patients with suspected COVID-19 all looked terrible - as if they were about to die at any second, often they did. Nobody talked to them due to the danger of aerosol generation and they were all too unwell to interact with each other. The nurses and healthcare assistants only approached patients if absolutely necessary. The patients lay there, gasping for breath, looking as if they would die at any second. Everyone on the ward continued their duties gowned up in protective equipment. Nobody spoke to each other. Relatives were not allowed in to see anyone. It was horrific, impersonal. Once he had finished in ITU, Kyle changed his protective equipment and moved into the COVID positive high dependency unit.

As he neared the bay, Kyle saw an older lady in a bed. She had an oxygen mask on and looked grey.

'H… help me.' She said, pulling her mask down

Kyle had been told not to approach patients and to simply continue to clean. He continued to scrub the ward. 'H… help me. I…I can't breathe.'

Underneath his protective equipment, Kyle could barely hear her. Unable to remove his equipment, he felt helpless.

'Just, come here, please, I can't hear you... in that mask.'

'I'm sorry, I… I can't. I'll get one of the nurses,' Kyle said, trying to make hand and arm gestures. He stopped mopping and went to the nursing station.

'The lady, the one in the second bed on the right, she keeps asking me to help her. What shall I do?'

'Nothing, she's COVID positive. Stay as far away as possible unless she needs something.'

'But… she looks like she needs help.'

'I know it's hard, but she's on oxygen, she's not fit for ITU. She's on a drip. There's nothing else we can do; we've been told to have as little contact with patients as we can, if we all get ill, who is going to look after them then?'

Disheartened, Kyle returned to his mop. The lady was reaching out towards him as he scrubbed around the bed.

'Help me… please,' she gasped.

After a time, Kyle edged over to her, closer than he dared to go.

'My son, please… just let me… speak to him… my phone, it's in the drawer.'

Kyle felt terrible. He should not be touching equipment belonging to COVID positive patients. But the lady seemed desperate, somehow.

Kyle went to walk off, then he paused. He had been given explicit instructions not to go near COVID positive patients. The nurses were not going to do anything. Kyle could understand why this was. They were already putting themselves at risk, but this was someone's gran, someone's mum. How could people just ignore her? All she wanted to do was to talk to her son. She wouldn't be able to speak much to him anyway due to the noise of the oxygen and the machines in the room. Maybe he could just get her phone for her? Kyle walked over to the unit by her bed and opened the drawer; her mobile was at the top. He took it out and placed it on the bed next to her.

'P… please, can you dial my son?'

No, there was no way that Kyle could dial the lady's son. He had already touched her phone. He shook his head. The lady took her mask off and picked the phone up. Kyle knew that he needed to go before someone saw him.

He changed his gloves and proceeded through the bay at the end of the ward. He made sure that he changed his protective equipment, cleaning the surfaces and mopping, all the time feeling guilty that he had stood so close to a patient with confirmed COVID-19. What if his protective equipment didn't work? What if he caught it? Gave it to his mum or grandad? Kyle began to feel that he had been really, really stupid, cringing every time someone walked nearer than two metres by him.

Once he had finished cleaning the ward, Kyle proceeded back through the bay. The nurses were at the bed of the lady who he had given the phone to. She was lying still in the bed clutching her phone. Kyle's heart dropped. He hoped that she had managed to get through to her son or putting himself and other people in danger like that would have all been futile.

'Excuse me, we're going to need someone to clean around the second bed in bay two in about ten minutes. Patient has passed away.'

Kyle nodded. As he walked past, he heard the nurse talking to one of the healthcare assistants.

'Yeah, died, she had just managed to phone her son. How she got that phone out is beyond me.'

Kyle kept on walking. He was seeing people dying every day. He remembered the first time that he had seen the man lying dead in his bed on his first shift. It had freaked him out, frightened him, he couldn't get the image of the man's face out of his mind. But now, it was almost as if it was becoming normal to him. How and when had that happened? He finished his job and went to leave the ward. One of the nurses was crying in the corner, trying to hide it. Kyle overheard one of the healthcare assistants asking her what was wrong.

'This,' she said. 'I bloody hate it. Why are we here? Only just been given protective equipment, We're putting our lives at risk? Being told one thing one minute then another the next! I can't cope.'

The feeling was sombre. Nobody was happy anymore, everyone in the hospital was miserable, uncertain. Kyle did his job and left a few hours later, feeling tired, unclean, and washed out. He tried to imagine what it was like for staff that had to stay for twelve or thirteen hours wearing masks and other protective equipment. But he couldn't. In the uncertainty, he could understand why they were fed up and resentful of the way that they had been treated.

10th May 2020

'Well, that was a waste of time! I might as well have just had a laugh!'

'What was?'

'We've just been told by the school to stop studying!'

The message from the school advised students that all final GCSE exam results would be based on predicted grades. Kyle was aggrieved. His teachers had all acknowledged that he had pulled his socks up, but he was sure that he could have done better in the final exams. Now it seemed as if all his hard work and new found diligence had been pointless.

Finding himself with little else to do, Kyle had been working extra shifts in the hospital. Apart from walking past the house and waving, or having a quick chat in the garden through the window, he had kept away from his grandad - especially after giving the lady with COVID her phone - and was really missing him.

Kyle had dared not meet his friends. Dressed in his protective equipment, he felt sure that he could not have caught anything from touching the lady's phone the other week and going close to her, but how could he ever be sure? Symptom-free, he was going for a walk to meet them up in the hills, taking care not to have contact with them and to avoid other people. The people of North Wales had been lucky that the weather had been so unusually dry and sunny. But it wasn't quite the same as going to school for the craic or just hanging out.

He began to dream back to the time when he was last happy. He longed to be chilling with Mo and his gang in someone's room, or studying with Roxanne, or most of all just being able to go and watch football with Grandad and go to Shone's café for a fry up after. Seeing him in the garden for a few minutes to drop off essential items just wasn't the same.

Sadly, the outcome for Grandad's neighbour Ned had not been good; one of the only good things to come from his death was the fact that it had finally made Grandad begin to take the restrictions a bit more seriously. Although still largely in denial, he no longer tried to pressure Kyle into going into the house for a cup of tea, or to stay for long periods of time in the garden. Grandad was quite clearly still not understanding the full seriousness of the situation.

After nearly two months of meeting to break the day up, he and his friends all acknowledged that they had become boring – nobody had anything new to tell anyone. And now, they couldn't even talk about their schoolwork because they weren't sitting their exams.

Then Mo had an idea. Once a week, he suggested that they should all learn something or teach each other something over Zoom. At first, Kyle felt apprehensive. He was sick of online learning, and staring at the computer. The first lesson was a painting lesson from Roxanne. Kyle had been on a socially distanced walk to his grandad's to borrow some of his watercolours. He planned to paint some pictures of the estate. Roxanne was going to show everyone how to do it. The next week, Mo taught everyone how to make rotis, which were a bit like chapatis. Kyle had no idea what to teach, so he did a high impact work out. It turned out to be fun, something different. But living at home with his mum wasn't such fun. Although they usually got on, spending an increasing amount of time together was not always easy.

'Kyle, will you get your clothes out of the washer? No, Kyle, not in the tumble dryer, on the line, it's a nice day, I'm not wasting electric on that.'

'Yeah, OK, Mum, get off my case. I washed some of yours too… you're welcome by the way.'

After he had bumped into Daryl by the park, Kyle had changed his route home. He now stuck to the heavily populated areas of the estates and the main roads. He remained hypervigilant while walking to and from work, attempting to take the most conspicuous route possible. Sooner or later he knew that he would encounter Daryl again. Although Daryl had still not come knocking at his door, Kyle felt sure that it was simply a matter of time.

'Eh, Kyle, you up for any more hours?' asked Michelle. 'Can you do up to your maximum?'

'Yeah, why not, not like I've got to study anymore, our exams have been cancelled.'

'Oh dear! Well, how are you going to pass them then?'

'We're all getting predicted grades apparently,' he said with a sigh.

'Aw, sounds like it's not going to be good then?'

The more he thought about it, the more Kyle was annoyed about his grades. He'd got a couple of As for design technology and English literature, Bs for maths and English language and Cs for the other subjects in his mocks.

'Well, I only got a couple of As and Bs, the rest were Cs, in my mocks anyway…'

Michelle's face dropped.

'Blimey, I didn't know that you were clever…'

Kyle frowned. 'What's that supposed to mean?'

'Well, it's just, you seem like a normal lad, not a swot, so you're clever then? Anyway, I've been asked again to see if anyone wants to go to the hospital up the coast. For some reason, they can't recruit. I've got some new cleaners starting here next week so I've been asked to see if anyone wants to go.'

'Na, not exactly clever. I could have and should have done a lot better in the real thing. No, I'm good about going to the coast, thanks.'

Working in the hospital when it was more heavily staffed was very different to working when there was a skeleton staff and little going on, it was a lot busier and a lot harder to do the job without interruption. And things had changed. Cleaning had become more of a priority in the hospital than ever before. By the end of the day, the sweat poured off him and he relished the moment that he could have a shower at the end of it.

Everyone was becoming used to the situation. Staff members' complacency was evident. It was as if all empathy and humanity had been lost. Acquiescence to this horrific situation had set in as an unspoken underlying culture. Because of the barriers in place, basic human presence and communication were missing. He shuddered as he thought about Grandad walking to the shop, or his mum forgetting to put her protective equipment on properly. Kyle worried even more now about being around COVID; this was the most horrible way to die. Kyle worried when he went home – what if he gave something to someone? One of his friends? Someone in the shop? Grandad, when he saw him in his garden? His friends thought that he was nuts when he insisted on staying two metres away from them when he saw them. So did Grandad when he wouldn't go into his house, or wiped down his shopping and things that he dropped off for him with antibacterial wipes, and socially distanced.

Today after work he was going to take some shopping over to Grandad. Because of the risks, he usually went home first and wiped all the shopping down. Then, he made his own flask of tea to take just in case. Trying to remember what shopping Grandad had asked for today, Kyle walked out of the hospital and into the car park.

'Alright, Kyle?'

Daryl!

Kyle turned around slowly to face him. 'Yeah?'

'Any more thoughts about coming back to work for us, Kyle?'

'No, none at all.'

'Come on… it's easy money, much easier than working in there.'

'I'm cleaning the COVID wards, Daryl. It might be hard going, but I'd rather die of COVID than be bumped off and put in the boot of a car.'

'Now, Kyle, come on, I'm a business man. Look, I don't know who has been talking, Kyle, but I think there's been a misunderstanding.'

'No, I don't think there has.'

'Well, I need help to run things, Kyle. I'm doing most of it on my own. A few of the others have been, shall we say, careless. Some have shot their mouths off. But not you, Kyle, I knew all along I could rely on you.'

'Daryl, it's not going to happen.'

'I'll be round to yours later, Kyle, and we'll have a bit of a chat about it shall we?'

'No, I think my mum would call the police; she doesn't know anything about you or the gang.'

'That would be very silly of her, wouldn't it, Kyle?'

'Yeah, but my mum, she doesn't know nothing. If she did, trust me, Daryl, she'd have gone to the police a long time ago.'

'We lost a lot of business in the fire, Kyle, a lot of business that I need to recuperate.'

Kyle shook his head and walked off.

'I know where you live, Kyle. I'll be seeing you soon, and I think it's time I paid your old mate Jason a visit, for telling little porkies about our organisation. People aren't very happy with him, Kyle.'

'I told you, man, I haven't seen Jason. And I don't owe you anything. So just leave me alone.'

'I'll be around, Kyle.'

Why couldn't he just leave him alone? It was as if he was just in a dream, a really bad dream, a nightmare, where there was nowhere that he could go to get away, and nothing that he could do about anything. What if Daryl did pay him a visit? What if he found out that Jason had seen him?

What if his mum called the police? The gang would want revenge. Kyle had to do something. And quickly. There was only one person that could help.

****

'How are you, Grandad?'

Grandad sighed loudly.

'To be honest, son, I'm sick of living like this. They've told me not to go out, but I don't care, I'm bloody going. I'm seventy-three, I could die next year, and I'm having to sit in this boring hole every day? I'm not dying driving myself mad! Not seeing anyone, spending my last living days holed up in the house like this; it's bloody ridiculous!'

Kyle sat down in Grandad's garden with trepidation. 'Sit down, son, I'll get you a brew. I'm bloody sick of all this - I'm not bloody shielding!'

'Grandad, you have to see it to believe it. I've seen some awful things in that hospital. People dying and everything. You really need to be careful going out and about. Don't make me one, I've got a flask.'

'God, what you doing, lad? I'll make you one!'

'What if I pass you droplets? It's too risky.'

'Aw, I couldn't give a toss anymore. If it's lasting indefinitely, I'm not just sitting in here on my own! I'll drive myself blooming mad! I'm not waiting till someone in that bloody government tells me I can go out. If I want to go out, I'll flaming well go!'

Typical Grandad. While most older people were sitting at home, petrified of COVID, Grandad was carrying on regardless. Even the death of his neighbour hadn't convinced him to remember to take care. Still, at least he was now wearing a mask when he went shopping. He was a constant worry to Kyle.

'If me time's up, me time's up. I might die anyway soon, and what for? Sitting 'ere on my own? I'll be careful, don't worry, but I'm not wasting my life.'

'Grandad! This time a few months ago, you were telling me how much worry I'd caused you and Mum, well, now it's the opposite, you're causing me nothing but worry. I'm seeing people die in there of this, and you're acting like it's not happening!'

'Yeah, alright, chill out. Anyway, I've got my mask now.'

'Well, start being more careful, and wearing it more often. And stop going to the shop. I can get you things.'

'There's no bloody need! I can…'

'Grandad, what part of this don't you understand? It's dangerous! Remember Ned? He just "went to the shop". For god sake, haven't you learned anything?'

'Anyway, forget all that nonsense, how are you?'

'Fed up too, Grandad. I think I need to get away from here.'

'Well, you know me and your mum spent all those years telling you that schooldays are the best days of your life, do you believe us now?'

Kyle was missing school. He was missing feeling productive, feeling that he was doing something with his life and seeing people. It was almost as if school had turned into his safe place, his haven, and now it had gone. Now he was all alone in the world, working in a hazardous environment on a daily basis, all the time watching his back for Daryl.

All week, Kyle felt bothered. He had felt bothered since he had seen Daryl; just knowing that he was around was disconcerting. It made him feel paranoid. He had been thinking about it a lot all week, especially since he had now stopped doing his school work. His job, wearing a mask and keeping away from people, stopped him from interacting with many people in work. Working longer hours, and doing the same repetitive tasks meant that he had time to think a lot about everything. During the day, his mum wasn't there so he had nobody except his friends to talk to. And there was only so much that he could tell them. He had been wondering if he should tell someone about Daryl - what if something happened?

Up until now, he hadn't told his mum much about the gang; about how they operated, about how dangerous they were. She was an obvious point of contact. If Daryl ever got to her, she could truthfully say that she knew nothing about it all. He didn't want to tell his friends, just in case any of them let it slip or it put them in a precarious position. The only other person that he had that he could feasibly tell was Grandad. Kyle knew that if he told Grandad, what he said would remain confidential, and he doubted that Daryl would come bothering a seventy-three-year-old man when he had no idea how close they were. It was clear from the comments that Daryl had made about Kyle's dad that he had no idea about the relationship that he had with his grandad.

'Anyway, Kyle, you're very quiet today. What's bothering you?'

'Grandad, do you remember when I got into that trouble? You know, when you posted the letter for me?'

Grandad nodded.

'The guy that I got into trouble about, I thought I'd seen the last of him. He's wanted by the police and he's back in the area. He looks desperate to recruit people for his business, probably because it's harder in lockdown, innit? I bumped into him the other week.'

'And? What did he say?'

'He told me that I had to start working for him again.'

'Well, what did you say?'

'I told him I didn't want to be in his gang, that those days were gone, but he wasn't having it, Grandad.'

'Oh.'

'I've seen him again today, he was even more insistent. Says he's coming round to my house. I can't have that, I can't have him coming anywhere near Mum.'

Grandad paused. He stared hard at Kyle for a few moments.

'There's only one way to get away from those types. You're going to have to lie low.'

'What? Where can I go?'

'You need to get away from him, Kyle. As far away as you can.'

'But where, Grandad? Come one, where can I go?'

Neither of them spoke.

'When Uncle Chris finishes his treatment in a month or two, maybe you could move to Devon for a bit with Auntie Moira?' said Grandad, eventually.

'I don't think I've got that long, Grandad. I can't think of anywhere else that I can go, not unless I make myself homeless.'

Then Kyle remembered something; why hadn't he thought of it before?

'My supervisor in work said something about moving to the other hospital up the coast. They're desperate for cleaners there apparently; she reckons I can stay up there.'

'If things are that bad, it doesn't sound like a bad idea. Maybe you should just do it? He can't just make you join his gang if you don't even live round here, can he? It's pointless for him. Maybe go and lie low for a few weeks until the heat dies down.'

11th May 2020

The gang sat in the field. It was a blazing hot day. Today, Eddie had joined them.

'The police were at Jade's yesterday, looking for Daryl. Apparently, he's been staying there,' said Mo.

'I heard he moved back in with Jade in her new flat, in Box Court. He was lying low, operating from there, apparently,' said Eddie. 'But someone rumbled him to the police; he's done a runner, but nobody knows where to.'

Kyle's blood ran cold and he felt the hairs on the back of his neck stand up on end. Daryl! So that's where he had been living all this time! At Jade's! Why, oh why couldn't he have been caught by the police last year? Had he been caught, that would have been the answer to all of Kyle's problems.

'All the county lines dealers are getting desperate round here, business is slow. It's hard to explain why a kid is travelling alone on a bus or a train; the risk of being stopped and searched is high,' said Mo.

Daryl was not only desperate, but brazen. He had somehow managed to evade the police and even move back in with Jade – right under their very noses!

'I thought they kidnapped Jade?' said Kyle, trying to hide the fact that he knew exactly what had happened to her. 'What's she doing letting him live with her again?'

'Yeah, after that, the rest of the gang got arrested, but, somehow, Daryl managed to split. He's still wanted by the police; she's that stupid, she let him come back.'

Jade, vulnerable and stuck in the spiral of addiction and desperate as usual. It would only take Daryl making her a short-term promise of supplying her with an immediate fix to worm his way into her flat.

'Shit, if he had nowhere else to stay except for Jade's he must be desperate,' said Roxanne.

'What about Jason?' asked Kyle.

'He's gone somewhere, nobody's seen him, not even Jade, apparently,' said Eddie.

'Shit,' muttered Kyle. 'Where?'

'They reckon he's gone to ground. Did one to Manchester a few months ago as soon as he learned that Daryl was back.'

When Daryl had returned, Kyle had tried to message Jason, but he hadn't been able to. He didn't have his number and, like Kyle, Jason was nowhere to be found on social media.

'Yeah,' said Mo. 'Daryl must be desperate if he's come back up here after the fire.'

Hearing that Daryl had moved from Jade's flat to an undisclosed location magnified Kyle's paranoia. Now he didn't know where he was. Where had Daryl gone? What was he doing? Could he see Kyle? Was he following him? Knowing that Daryl had been so close for all this time gave Kyle the creeps. But why had he not yet carried out his threats of forcing Kyle to re-join the gang?

'Jason's got a price on his head from what I've heard. Daryl thinks he's been talking. I wouldn't like to be Jason right now,' said Mo.

Dread and fear rose up in Kyle. If Daryl and his superiors ever found out about who had started the fire, Jason wouldn't be the only person that the gang wouldn't be happy with.

The next day, Kyle went to work. Sweating away in his hazmat, he scrubbed ITU. Some days he felt as if he was in a dream. The hazmat drowned out some of the noises from the machines and, even though it was uncomfortable, wearing so much equipment made him feel somehow invincible. Some days, feeling this way was the only thing that got Kyle through his shift. It was as if he was mopping away in his own little world. Today was an easier day; there was no movement in or out of ITU. All the beds were full.

There was only one patient in the non-COVID part of ITU. He was covered in tubes. There were bruises on his face. His leg was in plaster and he was heavily sedated. Whatever it was that had happened to him had not been good. Kyle hadn't seen much trauma in ITU since he had started working there; they said that it was mainly because there had been fewer car crashes, sporting injuries, fights and altercations since the start of the pandemic.

Working for longer periods of time in his hazmat was bearable unless he had to work quickly. Kyle could just about cope. This was always the case; just as he thought that his lungs would collapse, and he was empty of all the sweat that his body could produce, Kyle's shift finished and it was time to remove his protective clothing. Doing this job was making him more and more determined, that even if he failed every single one of his exams, he would go back and re-sit them so that he could do something with his life.

With ineffable relief, Kyle returned to the changing room to take his hazmat off. As he did so, two of the nurses were stood talking in the entrance. Kyle couldn't help overhearing their conversation.

'How's the young lad in there today? The one who was left for dead.'

'Not great last time I heard. The police were down here yesterday making enquiries. They reckon it's all drugs related.'

Kyle's heart dropped at the mention of drugs and assault. Even with COVID-19, drug gangs were still functioning. He wondered who the young lad was and what had happened to him. Left for dead? He looked in a really bad way. Seven months ago, that could have very easily have been him.

Later that day, Kyle met up with Mo in the field.

'You heard about Jason?'

'No.'

'He came back to Jade's thinking that the coast was clear. He got found by Daryl and half-murdered. They beat him up and dumped him in the back of the park in the middle of the night. Nobody found him 'til the next day. They thought he was dead. He's in ITU.'

Kyle's heart stopped beating. His blood froze and ran cold. Jason? That had been Jason lying there in intensive care! Kyle would never have recognised him! Daryl must have felt sure that at some point he would come back to Jade's, and he, or someone else, had just waited. If Kyle didn't agree to re-join the gang, that could be him lying there in a few weeks. Or worse still, being carried out in a body bag.

12th May 2020

'Er, Michelle, can I have a word?'

'Yeah, sure, what about?'

'Well, I've been thinking about what you asked, about swapping to the other site.'

'Well, yeah,'

'It's just, I could do with getting away for a bit.'

'Oh? Why the sudden change of heart?'

Kyle paused. Everyone that knew him knew about his previous involvement with Daryl and his gang. If he was going to do this properly, he would have to be honest.

'Can I talk to you about something? And will you promise not to tell my mum?'

'Well, maybe, go on…'

Kyle relayed the story to Michelle of how he had become involved with Daryl, about how he had managed to evade him when Jade's house had mysteriously burned down and about how Daryl was now attempting to re-recruit him to be involved in drug dealing. And finally about his new threats, and the fact that Jason was now lying unconscious in an ITU bed.

'Jeez, Kyle. What's your mum said about it all?'

'Haven't told her about the last bit.'

'Well, how on earth are you going to keep that from her? You know, if they come knocking at your door?'

'I don't know. But I need to, I can't get her involved.'

'Well, if it's as bad as you say, what I suggest you do is get a transfer from the agency, and then when they ask for a reference, I'll just have to tell them that your name is, I dunno, Cuthbert or somat.'

'Cuthbert?'

'Well, I dunno, something. Give me a better one then?'

'Clarke Kent? Or Idris Elba?'

'Yeah, yeah, we'll think of something! Just not the name you go by; if you call yourself Kyle, they'll all know who you are in that hospital.'

'B… but where would I stay? I'd have to find digs and all that…'

'Well, there's the hospital accommodation, nothing special, but you can stay if you're a keyworker just for service charge… plus they'll pay more. I'll make some enquiries.'

Kyle's face hit the fresh air as he emerged from the hospital. He squinted as his eyes became accustomed to the daylight.

Kyle had made his mind up - he would need to leave town sooner than later. But he had to speak to his mum later when she got back from work.

'Mum, I've got to go away for a bit.'

His mum stopped making dinner.

'You what, Kyle? What do you mean, go away for a bit?'

'I just need to get out of town.'

His mum put her head in her hands. 'Kyle, what for? Is this some sort of a joke? Are you having a laugh?'

Kyle shook his head. 'No, Mum. I'm not.'

'Well, where are you going? And why? You've behaved for months; it's lockdown so you can't possibly be getting up to anything, all you've done is work, so what's the problem?'

'Look, Mum, it's to do with, you know, before, stuff that I got involved in that I shouldn't have. The person who I thought had gone, he's come back!'

'Oh.'

'I need to go somewhere where he won't come looking for me.'

'Kyle, are you going to tell me what the flaming heck is going on?'

Kyle shook his head. 'No, Mum. But all you need to do is not mention anything about me to anyone. Just say I've disappeared and you don't know where I've gone.'

'What's happened? You were doing so well! I thought you'd turned a corner and…'

Kyle was going to have to come clean.

Kyle sighed. 'Look, it's to do with earlier in the year, the trouble I got myself into. I thought it had gone away, but it hasn't. He's already threatened me, I mean the guy that I used to work for, and now he's on the run from the police, he's trying to make me carry packages with drugs in them again.'

His mum drew a deep breath. 'Hell fire, Kyle! What on earth have you got yourself into here?'

'Hopefully nothing, not if I lie low for a bit. Look, I've got a plan, OK?'

'Kyle, I don't think I can cope with this!' His mum began to sob. 'Why don't you just, I dunno, go to the police?' she asked as tears rolled down her cheeks.

'Mum, he's nuts, he'll kill me if I do that. There's an ex-runner lying in an ITU bed in the hospital as we speak. Plus, I don't know who else is involved, if there's anyone higher than him that'll just be gunning for me if I dob him in. Plus, if he goes to jail, he'll get out one day, and then what? And if you don't know where I am, you can't tell them, can you? Look, you've got to trust me, OK?'

'Well, where you gonna go? What you gonna do?'

'I'm not going to tell you where I'm going, Mum. If you don't know, you can't say anything, can you?'

'But… but what if something happens to you?'

'Look, Mum,' said Kyle, putting his arms around her, 'nothing will, you've just got to trust me, OK?'

'But…how can you afford to…'

'It's sorted.'

Much as he tried to persuade her, Kyle's mum just couldn't understand what was happening or why he needed to go. As far as she was concerned, Kyle could tell that she thought that everything was sweet; he was no longer involved with the gang, he had got his head down, he had behaved and that was that. But as Mo had told him right at the start, thinking that he could ever just leave the gang wasn't the case and never would be – why hadn't he listened?

There were a couple of other people that he needed to phone. First he called Mo.

'Mo, I'm going away for a bit, lying low until I know it's safe.'

'But mate, where are you…'

'Trust me, mate, if you don't know, it's better for everyone. I'll be back, buzz you in the next couple of days, OK? Just tell the others I'm lying low and I'll Facetime everyone next week.'

Next he needed to talk to Grandad.

'Grandad?'

'Yeah?'

'You know what we talked about? Daryl? Well he's on the run from the police again, apparently he was hiding at Jade's flat. I'm off, I'm staying up at the other hospital for a bit.'

'Oh.'

'I'm staying in the hospital accommodation, it's not far from Cliff's lighthouse. Please keep it to yourself.'

15th May 2020

The weather was glorious as Kyle stepped off the train. Not that it mattered – it wasn't like the last time that he had visited this part of the world with Grandad in the summer. Shops were shut, the town centre desolate. The summer adornments of buckets, spades, floats and other items outside the shops weren't there to distract from the otherwise forlorn exteriors of the shops.

The room in the hospital accommodation was basic and grim. The walls, doors and ceilings were clinically white, just like the main hospital building. Grey industrial cushion floor adorned the floors and corridors, like a sea of dirty water running through. The room that he was staying in was dingy. It contained a single bed, a sink and a wardrobe. If the wardrobe hadn't have looked as if it had been rescued from a skip thirty plus years ago, it could have been mistaken for a side room in the main hospital.

The whole place had a bizarre, unclear NHS timing system. Kyle could not fathom why it was that the heating sometimes came on in the middle of the night and not in the day. It made no sense as the weather was sweltering. The draughty pre-war windows were black with mould around the poorly-sealed edges. The radiator pipes clanged, and spluttered, struggling every time that someone ran the hot water pipes, trying to fill the bath with the cracked stained grouted 1970s tiles, or the heating came on. It was surprisingly dim inside given that the weather was so bright outside. The fact that someone could design a building that let in so little light when there was so much outside was a conundrum in itself. Quite frankly, it was depressing.

Once he had got there, Kyle had realised that he was hideously unprepared. He had assured his mum that he had packed, but having never had to pack for himself before he had brought an insufficient amount of items. He had a couple of spare uniforms which he would need to wash on a daily basis in the pre-paid machine. Furthermore, he had been limited on what he could carry and bring with him on the train. Apart from his toiletries, a few changes of clothes, socks and underwear and a "cookbook for students" that his mum had packed him, he had little else.

Kyle had not brought anything to eat. He had a flick through the cook book that his mum had sent up with him. The first recipe that he came across was for tuna pasta bake. He decided that he would give it a go. Except for beans on toast and sandwiches, Kyle had never really cooked anything at home.

He took a stroll into town. There was nowhere open and nothing to do except explore the desolate streets. Alone, this was boring. Kyle made his way to the supermarket. He bought himself some ingredients to make his tea with and then made his way back to the accommodation. It was all surreal, and lonely. But at least he felt safe. He no longer needed to look over his shoulder.

It seemed that Kyle was the only regular occupant of the building except for the occasional comings and goings of other people. Most of them appeared to be working nights and sleeping in the day. Given that he was classed as a keyworker, he was getting his accommodation at a reduced rate paying service charge only. Kyle felt glad about this; he didn't feel that the accommodation was worthy of rent. Or indeed a service charge which included heating in one of the hottest months of the year. Had he had to pay full price for it, he would have considered himself robbed. He had booked back to back cleaning shifts for his maximum hours for the next two weeks, realising that otherwise he would have nothing else to do except sit and think.

Kyle had picked up a newspaper. He finished off his tea in the grubby little kitchen. He opened his paper. And there, inside, was a picture of Daryl. The headline read "Man on the run for attempted murder".

28th May 2020

'Evan, you've not done the surfaces yet, you need to move quicker,' yelled Neil, Kyle's new boss.

Kyle continued cleaning, oblivious to the fact that he was being addressed.

'Evan, Evan!'

Kyle jumped as the penny finally dropped: Evan, his new name was Evan.

'Yeah?' replied Kyle.

'Have you got hearing problems or something? The surfaces, you haven't done them!'

'Yes, I have, I did them first.'

Kyle always did the surfaces first before cleaning the floors just as Michelle had taught him. She said that the rubbish dropped onto the floor and that could be cleaned later.

'Right, well, you should have finished it all by now, let's go,' he said, clapping his chubby hands together as he ordered Kyle about. Sweat dripped through Neil's hair net from his greasy comb-over as he marched off to the next section of the hospital, failing to even check that Kyle had, in fact, cleaned the surfaces.

Neil was an overweight, fifty-something man who did not speak nicely to people. Kyle had never seen a smile cross his downcast face, which had all the hallmarks of premature ill health. He was a sharp contrast to Michelle who was approachable, kind and likeable; Neil's management style was autocratic. He gave out orders in an unnecessarily rude manner. Consequently he was immensely disliked by his workforce. Kyle and Neil had not got off to a good start. It was becoming evident as to why the hospital had recruitment issues for the cleaning department.

In order to remain elusive, Kyle had told everyone that his name was Evan. Every time Neil called him in his usual obstinate manner demanding an immediate response, Kyle failed to respond. It took him a few days to remember that he was now called Evan. This angered Neil, who demanded that his orders were carried out straight away

Neil didn't get involved in doing any work. He failed to muck in and help like Michelle did when they were short-staffed, or asked to deep clean areas for largely unforeseen reasons which subsequently increased the usual workload. Neil simply stood back and yelled orders, ranting at everyone until the work was completed. Had he rolled up his sleeves and helped, tasks would undoubtedly have taken less time to complete, therefore his approach to the situation appeared futile and entirely pointless to Kyle. Kyle contemplated advising him to address this, but he quickly realised that Neil was not someone who was amenable to advice and couldn't be approached. Kyle wasn't enjoying working for Neil: time passed slowly.

At first, Kyle's main goal was to put as much distance between himself, Daryl and whoever else had been recruited to the gang as possible. He lived for the group chats and Facetime with his friends and his mum. He missed Grandad who he could only speak to on the phone - this was what kept Kyle going in his most lonely moments. However, after a while, even this didn't make him feel any less lonely than he already did.

The accommodation had a day room with a flowered carpet and chairs that looked as though they belonged in a 1960s school staff room. Kyle pulled at the doors of the faded G Plan cabinet. Apparently it contained jigsaws and books. It was locked shut. Of course it was! How had he even thought that it might be open due to the risk of spreading the virus?

Every afternoon after work, Kyle followed the same pattern. He went for a walk or a run, then wandered into town to buy supplies for his tea, trying to choose a different recipe out of the cookbook every night. Even though his cooking skills had improved, he couldn't make too much food: he had nobody to share it with. But still, it gave him something to do, a challenge to look forward to. In the paper, the main news was the same as it had been for the last few months. The front pages consistently spouted figures and other depressing statistics about the virus and how many lives it had claimed. There was literally nothing else that he could do and nowhere that he could go.

With little else to think about, Kyle often ruminated over it all; about how lonely he was, the fact that he had nearly ruined his life, the shame and worry that he had brought on his mum and grandad, the guilt. Now, he was being further punished by being forced to have predicted grades for his exams; the exams that he had worked so hard for!

As time went on, odd thoughts filled his head. Alone, with no friendly faces, often in the midst of loneliness, Kyle's mind became irrational. Maybe he had deserved what had happened? Maybe he deserved to be murdered by Daryl because of all the misery that he had brought on everybody else? At night, he would wake up at all kinds of odd hours in a cold sweat, convinced that Daryl was there. The longer that time went on, the longer it took to pass and Kyle became increasingly convinced that he was being watched.

Every time he thought about Daryl, which, alone, with little else to do, was a lot, Kyle felt anxious. He wondered what Daryl would do to him if he caught up with him, a non-compliant "Bic", who had decided to leave the gang. Would he be put into the boot of a car and rolled into a quarry? Or shot? Stabbed? His body disposed of never to be seen again? Poisoned to death? The myriad of possibilities were endless as was the time that Kyle had to ruminate over it all.

Then Kyle went to work and that was depressing. Unlike his previous job, there was no team spirit and he didn't mix with the other staff. Nobody seemed to speak to each other or have any kind of relationship. Despite the job being near enough the same, the culture was very different mainly due to Neil's management style. Consequently, everyone was miserable. Because nobody there was as friendly as they were in his old hospital, he felt even more isolated. Working in such a miserable environment gradually began to take its toll.

Still, he saw and heard the stories of the people that hadn't made it. Every day the front page of the paper proclaimed how many new victims of the virus there were and then there were the stories of people who had lost family, friends and people that they loved. And Kyle was reminded of how lucky he was.

Maybe he should just go back home to his family and carry on regardless, despite Daryl? If he was on the run, surely he wouldn't be so brazen as to turn up at Kyle's house? But then if he was desperate, what if he did? He was a psychopath who had half-murdered Jason, why would he not do the same to Kyle? As he went over things, Kyle felt guilt, guilt that it had happened to someone else, and disappointment. Why had he been so stupid? He was just a stupid kid who aspired to be something more than he was. Someone vulnerable to draw in with the promise of money, and status.

He tried to remind himself about the good things. If he hadn't encountered Daryl, he would have probably ended up failing or not being entered for many of his exams anyway as he was not doing any work in school. What if he had got involved with a gang when he was older? The consequences could have been so much worse. He would have not started behaving, and made his mum proud of him. He would not have seen people like Daryl for who they were, and the promise of an easy fix as something that in fact perpetuated problems that should be avoided. He would not have had as much respect for his mum and grandad and appreciated what good people they were, and concentrated on being a good person himself. He would probably have not got himself a job, and made new friends like Roxanne. He would still be smoking and taking drugs in the park with aspirations that reached no further than the end of the estate.

Kyle made his way back to town. He needed to buy some food. As he emerged from the supermarket, he walked down the pavement back towards the path. A lad slightly younger than him pulled into the car park on a bicycle. There was something about him that made Kyle notice him. He reminded him of someone; the latest Adidas trainers, swish new mobile phone on which he was dialling someone's number, latest clothes. But he looked bothered, haunted. A car pulled into the car park, pulled up next to the boy and he leaned down to speak to the driver, handing him something. And Kyle realised exactly why he recognised him: he was looking at himself, eight months ago.

Kyle's heart stopped as he dared to look at the kid, the kid with the sallow sunken face, dressed in his best Adidas gear, with the new trainers and bike, but with his very soul long since sucked out of him. Kyle wondered at what point of the cycle he was in? He looked too despondent to be in the initial honeymoon period where he was loving his new job. Not quite burned out enough to be at the later end where he was only good enough for treatment such as that doled out to people like Jade and Jason; no, he was somewhere in the middle, at the point where he, Kyle, had forcibly removed himself. Kyle hoped that he had a house that he could burn down, without being caught. Otherwise, the kid was heading for certain disaster. It wasn't just where Kyle lived, it was here too: drugs and gangs were everywhere. Without turning back around for a final glance, Kyle continued out of the car park and walked off in the direction of the costal path.

That evening he went for a run. He ran into the town and up to the lighthouse. Kyle hoped that Cliff would be around; the last few times that he had run up there he hadn't seen him. As luck would have it, there he was.

'Cliff,' he called. Cliff waved back to him.

The tide was low so Kyle hopped over the rocks towards where Cliff was.

'Good to see you, Kyle. How you doing?' asked Cliff.

'Er, yeah, not bad.'

Cliff made Kyle a cup of tea and they sat on the rocks below the lighthouse, two metres apart, chatting. For the first time in a week or so, with the wind whistling through his hair, and inhaling the salty sea air, Kyle felt happy, and alive. Kyle had not spoken to anyone that he knew or had any kind of connection with on a face-to-face basis for some time - it was nice to be able to sit and chat to a friendly face.

'So how's your grandad? I haven't spoken to him for a few weeks.'

'He's fine. He's just getting on with it. You know what he's like, out and about when he wants to go, refusing to shield or stay in because he doesn't believe in any of it.'

Cliff laughed. He knew Kyle's grandad well.

'And what brings you down here?'

'Er… well… I'm working.'

'Where?' You travelling every day?'

'Er no, I'm staying up here.'

Cliff met Kyle's stare with incredulity. 'Really? Why up here? Why not at home with everyone else?'

Kyle's silence spoke volumes.

'You're in trouble again, Kyle, aren't you?'

Kyle nodded. 'Kind of. It's someone I ran some jobs for at the beginning of the year. I was stupid, Cliff. I started transporting packages for a gang. Thought I'd only do it for a couple of weeks, to get some cash. So stupid! I left coz it was awful.'

'So you thought that was the end of it, and now they're back?'

Kyle nodded. 'Yeah. I hadn't seen or heard from any of them for months, I thought it was over, but it wasn't. It's all my own fault, Cliff, I was easy fodder, stupid. The main guy that I've got beef with is wanted for attempted murder.'

Cliff nodded. 'Oh dear.'

'Yeah, so I've tried to get my head down, you know, study, and keep out of trouble. It was working. I did my mocks, did well. Then I started working, cleaning with Mum in the hospital over lockdown. And he's reappeared. So I left.'

'Well, you want to watch that they don't find out that you're up here, mate, this area is rife for drugs, they're everywhere. It's got good transport links.'

'I know. I guess it all comes down to two choices, Cliff, ride it out and try and keep my head down, or go back home and get my head bent. Please don't tell anyone you've seen me.'

24th June 2020

Kyle stuck it out for another few weeks before he buckled. He couldn't stand not seeing his mum, grandad and friends any longer. It seemed like a lifetime since he had last seen any of his family or friends in person. He was beginning to dream of his life back home as if it only existed in a mythical far away land. He would give anything to be back in his mum's arms, to have a cup of tea with his grandad again, to chill with his friends. He lived for the afternoons that he met with Cliff and helped him with odd bits that he could do outside. Sometimes Cliff was merely grateful for a hand with the heavy equipment. It had been the only thing that had kept him sane for the past few months.

Today, Kyle had made his mind up. He was taking a carefully planned trip back home. He deliberated and debated about whether or not he should go… surely he wouldn't be so unlucky as to bump into Daryl if he only went for a couple of days and kept his head down? Would he? Besides, if Daryl was wanted for murder, surely back home in town would be the last place he would be. Kyle figured that not much harm could come about. He texted his mum.

'Mum, I'm coming back for the night. I miss you.'

Kyle wasn't working for the next two days. Home was just under an hour away in the car, just under two on the train. Already it seemed like another world away from where he was. He would stay with Mum for the night, and then spend a bit of time with his grandad. Maybe he would even be able to meet up with the gang somewhere quiet and then catch the evening train back up the coast for work on Monday. Kyle finished his shift and caught the last train back to town.

He disembarked and looked around. The town seemed smaller somehow, but fresher, nicer. Kyle hadn't realised how homesick he was until he inhaled the familiar smells of the town air as he walked towards home; the chippy, the fumes from the traffic, the laundrette, the kebab shop… how he had missed this place. He tried to keep to the more secluded and inconspicuous paths and roads as he made his way back towards the estate.

'Mum, I'm home.'

'Kyle, come here.' She pulled him into her arms.

Kyle held his mum for what seemed like a lifetime. He didn't want to let her go. It was lovely; it was just like she used to hold him when he was little. He felt safe in her arms. He loved her so much! Paranoid as he was about passing something onto her, she was as protected and as at risk as he was – not seeing her for all this time had been worth it for just one hug.

Kyle sat cuddled up to his mum, drank tea, ate rubbish and watched films until the early hours of the morning. Careful not to disclose to her exactly where he was, they talked all night; he told her about the terrible accommodation, about Neil, about his cooking. So that she didn't know exactly where he was, there were aspects that Kyle did not dare to tell her about, such as how he had met up with Cliff, or what job it was that he was doing.

They ended up laughing about the whole situation. She reiterated to him that it was temporary. With someone to regulate his thoughts, his feelings, his emotions, Kyle felt much better

'Well, it looks like I'm stuck cleaning. There are no other jobs that I can get to anywhere,' said his mum.

'Well, what do you want to do?'

'I've been thinking a lot; I really think that I'd like to be a teacher, Kyle.'

'Really?'

'Yeah. I used to quite enjoy helping you with your work. I'm going to look into it.'

'OK, I'll make you a deal.'

'Go on.'

'If I pass my exams, we can go to college together.'

'I'll have a good look at it.'

Tomorrow was Saturday. Kyle planned to spend time with Grandad. He would see his friends on Sunday before making his way back up to the coast. The Sunday hours of the trains meant that he was limited regarding what time he could get back. Kyle got up early, pulled his hood up and made his way to Grandad's.

'Grandad,' Kyle called as he went up his drive to the back of the house.

'Mate! I've missed you, come here,' said Grandad, going to give Kyle a hug.

'No, no way, Grandad. It's still not safe.'

'Yeah, but they're relaxing it all, it's going, isn't it?'

'No, it's just come down with the social distancing. I've missed you, Grandad.'

'Well, sit down, have a brew, tell me all about your new job.'

Kyle sat down in Grandad's garden and got his flask of tea out. He began to tell him all about it; the dire accommodation, how lonely he was, and about Neil.

'You should see him, Grandad, the guy is a total tool.'

'I'd rather you than me, I'd have decked him by now.'

'Yeah, you definitely would have.'

'So, when you coming home?'

'I don't know. I really want to, but I don't know. I suppose when I know that Daryl's not here.'

'You never know, son, maybe he's stuck here, until lockdown's lifted a bit,' said Grandad. 'You're probably best off staying out of the way. I've seen that Daryl in the paper, he might still be round here, he was right under their noses last time and they didn't realise.'

Grandad had a point.

Kyle spent the rest of the afternoon with Grandad in the garden. He helped him to dig and weed at the back where nobody would notice him. That evening, he ordered his mum an Indian takeaway. After, they sat up talking, with a few beers. It was the first time that Mum had let him drink in the house. It was like sitting up with Roxanne, or Mo, or someone who was his friend, his best friend. The next morning, Kyle arranged to meet up with the gang in the field up the mountain before he left for the coast.

He walked through the estate with his hood up. On this glorious day, the streets were full of people, walking their dogs, meeting for chats, doing not a lot else; just procrastinating and pondering and making up their own theories about the virus. He headed up into the hills where he met the rest of the gang.

'Kyle! Sod the social distancing,' Roxanne screamed as she went to throw her arms around him, closely followed by Mo and Eddie

'Rox, don't! I don't want to pass you something.'

Reluctantly, they settled for an elbow bump.

Kyle had made a flask of coffee, Mo had a flask of tea, Roxanne had made scones. Eddie had brought cigarettes. Kyle sat there, feeling like a free man.

'So why did you do one, man?' asked Roxanne.

'Well, I suppose I just felt like a change of scene.'

Roxanne looked up at him, incredulous. 'Nothing to do with Daryl being around, and what happened to Jason?'

Kyle didn't reply.

'Thought so,' said Roxanne. 'Why didn't you just tell us? It's obvious anyway. What do you think we were going to do? Dob you in?'

'No,' said Kyle. 'It's just, well, you know. If you don't know, if anyone comes asking, you can't tell them and get into any hassle yourself. Anyway, the shit I could be in is that serious, I don't really want anyone to know where I've gone – not just for my sake, for everyone else's.'

Mo didn't speak. Kyle could tell that Mo had probably, out of everyone, worked out exactly where it was that he had gone.

'Anyway, how is Jason?'

'Woken up, he's on a ward now. Too shit scared to talk to the police though,' said Eddie.

Kyle felt relief. At least Jason had woken up. But how long for? What if Daryl went after him again?

For a time, Kyle sat in the sun on the top of the hill with his friends, and an odd warm sensation in his heart. Just for a few hours, he felt free of worry. He didn't need money, or to buy anything, or to go to the cinema or the fast food restaurant, he just needed his mum, his grandad, and his friends, the people that he loved, the ones that he could trust. He'd had an awesome afternoon. Now he could go back and handle work for another few weeks.

At the end of the afternoon, Kyle bid his friends goodbye. He was awash with melancholy as he contemplated not being able to see them for some time. But the whole point of him lying low was so that he wouldn't be noticed. Sooner or later, word would get round the estate that he had come back. Someone would have seen him or noticed that he was home. What if Daryl found out?

With a heavy heart, he headed towards the train station, dreading returning to his accommodation and going back to work with Neil. Back there, it was lonely, and miserable. He knew that for now he would miss his family and his friends. Zoom just wasn't the same. As he ruminated over the knowledge that Daryl was still around, paranoia set in as he thought about what might happen, if Daryl saw any of his friends; what if he cross examined them? And found all the WhatsApp messages on someone's phone? Maybe for the time being, he needed to go even deeper undercover.

The further that he walked into town, the further away from familiarity and from where he felt safe, the more paranoid Kyle became. Then, just as he neared the station, a car pulled up next to him. Kyle dared not look at the driver, he had already seen enough: the front of the car was the battered jalopy that Daryl had been driving last time that he had seen him. Feeling panicked, needing to do something, anything to keep him occupied, Kyle pulled his phone out and pretended to look at it. Thoughts of the worst case scenario began to flash through Kyle's mind: this was the moment he had dreaded. Then he had an idea. He waited with trepidation.

'Alright, Kyle? I've bin looking for you, you seem to be avoiding me.'

'Yeah, hi, Daryl.'

'I heard you were back. Where are you off?'

'Aw, just into town.'

'What for, Kyle? There's nowhere open.'

'Well, just for a walk.'

'Well, if you've got spare time, I've got a lucrative job for you here.'

'Na.'

'Where are you really going, Kyle? With a rucksack? Thinking of catching a bus or a train? Or staying somewhere else?'

Daryl had evidently been finding out about Kyle and what he was doing. Kyle wondered if he knew that he was home. Had someone seen him? Had one of his mates slipped up? Kyle had tried so hard to keep his visit a secret. Maybe Daryl had just dropped lucky and seen him walking up the road. But the feeling of not being able to trust everyone was gut wrenching.

'Get in, come for a drive with me.'

Kyle shook his head.

'Na, mate. I'm not interested anymore, sorry.'

'You can't just leave, Kyle.'

'Like I said, I'm not interested, I've found an alternative job. Working conditions and pay are much better. So thanks, but no thanks.'

Kyle carried on walking, pretending to be unfazed by Daryl's menacing tone and demeanour. Daryl drove next to him.

'I said get in, Kyle.'

'No.'

'Now.'

'No.'

'Now, Kyle.'

'What for, Daryl? Because you want me to go back to drug dealing for you? So that you can kill me, like you kill other kids when you're done with them?'

Daryl's face turned to thunder. 'Aw, poor Jason. He won't be able to blab for a bit, at least not when I get hold of him next time, I'll finish him off properly then; now, if you don't want the same thing to happen to you, get into the car.'

'Na, mate. Never again.'

Daryl's eyes narrowed. Sweat began to pour down Kyle's forehead. He hoped that the video was recording. He just needed a few more nuggets.

'Get in, Kyle, or you'll be very sorry!'

'Na,' said Kyle again, calling Daryl's bluff. The street wasn't empty. There were people milling around on their way home from work, doing their hourly exercise. Daryl would need to be stupid to fire a gun or stab him.

'You've been avoiding me, Kyle. Where have you been? Because you haven't been at home now, have you? And none of your little friends have seen you. So where is it that you've been?'

'I don't live here anymore, man. Maybe go and recruit someone who does.'

'Na, you made a lot of money for us, Kyle, you think I'm just gonna let you go?'

This was better, much better.

'Yeah, selling drugs in the packets? Like the other kids you recruited? What is it you call us? Bics?'

'It's a business opportunity, Kyle.'

'Yeah, selling drugs for your county lines business. The one you run down in Hereford as well? And then chuck the kids you're done with into a quarry outside Oswestry in the boot of your car so they just "disappear"?'

'Like I said before, Kyle, you know too much. I'm going to give you one last chance to get in the car…'

'A few kids have gone missing, and you were one of the last people to see them, Daryl. Everyone knows. You're wanted by the police, aren't you, Daryl? It's just a matter of time.'

Daryl stared coldly at Kyle, as if he wanted him dead, there and then.

'Listen, you little punk, that's it, now get in the car or I'll kill you…'

'To be honest, I don't care anymore, Daryl. I'd actually rather you did kill me than come back and work for you.'

'Well, maybe I'm just going to have to shut you up then, Kyle, you little shit. You've asked for it. No one is going to miss you, Kyle, it's time I shut you up for good.'

Kyle caught a glint in the sunlight. A glint of metal – a gun. 'One day, Kyle, when you're least expecting it, when you're on your own, or walking somewhere, you'll wish that you'd shown me a bit more respect.' Daryl was pointing the gun straight at him. 'I'll find you, Kyle, and I'll be watching, then "bang", you're dead meat.'

Kyle looked around him. There were people in the street. Just a few more metres…

'Yeah, see you later, Daryl.'

And with that, Kyle hopped over the adjoining railings and onto the path below, leaving Daryl in the car above. As he landed back on the ground with the familiar taste of sweat on his lips, his heart pounded in his chest as he clicked the "record" button off on his phone. Quickly, he disappeared into the undergrowth that led back to the park.

'Kyle…Kyle.'

When Kyle was younger, jumping off the barriers of the flyover had once been one of his favourite pass-times. It was where Eddie had broken his leg. As much as his mum had scolded him when she had found out what he had been doing, it had turned out to be an essential life skill. But he needed to leave town, now!

Daryl's cries grew fainter the further Kyle ran.

Maybe he had been stupid to come back. One thing was for sure, Daryl appeared to believe that somehow, he, Kyle, was Daryl's property to use as he pleased. And now Kyle had said too much, it was obvious that he was a liability to Daryl and he needed to be silenced.

Kyle sank into an alleyway as he left the undergrowth and walked towards the train station. He paused before he came back to the road, and played the recording back on his phone. It was perfect! Daryl's face was clear, his threats could be heard word for word. Somehow, he just needed to get Daryl's phone number and forward him the video. Kyle called the only person that he knew that would know what to do with it.

'Grandad, he's caught up with me. He's just pointed a gun at me. I've just sent you a video of him. In case anything happens to me, keep it safe until I can let him know I've got it so he'll leave me alone.'

Grandad took a deep breath on the other end of the phone.

'Jeez, Son! OK, I'll watch it now. Just give me a minute.'

A minute later, Grandad rang Kyle back.

'Yeah, right, I see him. Listen, son, he's going to try and kill you. I think you should call the police now.'

'No, Grandad, there are others, if I dob him in, I'm dead meat. I'm gonna keep my head down until the next train.'

'No, son, leave it, get the one after that. He'll be expecting you to be on it. You're just gonna have to hide out somewhere, stay somewhere for an hour and get the last one back.'

'You're right.'

'Phone me when you're on the train.'

Kyle stayed out of sight for what seemed like hours; thinking, planning, contemplating. Eventually, it was time. If he was to get the final train of the day, he needed to go now. He looked at his phone; he had ten minutes left until it was due. Looking slightly odd on such a warm sunny evening, he walked swiftly down the back alleys in the direction of the train station, avoiding the main roads. As Kyle emerged from the back streets of town and turned into the street before the train station, he proceeded with trepidation, staying in the shadows of the buildings just outside, using the least visible route. All the time, he kept one eye on the cars driving up and down the road, wondering if Daryl's was one of them. Kyle shrank back into the unkempt shrubbery in the front of the building in front of the train station. He had to get on the next train! He had to get away!

The platform that he needed to get the train from was visible from the road. If he went and stood there, waiting, he would be a sitting duck. There was only one place that Kyle could go where he could wait for the train and not be seen by Daryl. Cautiously, he crossed over the main road. He had two minutes until the train pulled in. Thankfully the announcement advised that it was on time. Kyle sat halfway down the train station steps out of sight of the road, pretending to look at his phone, praying that Daryl would not park up in his car and take a walk to the platform.

Paranoid, he ran through every eventuality of what might happen. What if Daryl knew where he was going and was waiting at the other end of the line for him? What if he had seen him cross the road? No, he was just being stupid – he had driven off. What if he had spies?

The train was just pulling in. Kyle waited until he saw the other passengers get off and then proceeded down the steps and got on, scanning the area as he did so. Daryl was nowhere to be seen. Passengers and people mulling around the station were few and far between. There was nobody on the road, and no suspicious-looking cars around. He hoped and prayed that Daryl hadn't seen him. He went into the toilet as soon as he got on so that should Daryl be watching him at a distance he would not see him in any of the carriages.

He waited until the train pulled off out of sight of the station and the main road, and left the toilet.

'Travelling only for business at the moment,' said the ticket inspector.

Kyle nodded. 'For work.' He showed the conductor his ID badge for the hospital, paid his fare and got his ticket. He remained standing and went into the toilet as the train stopped at the next few stops out of town. Eventually, as the train sped into the open countryside and away from town, Kyle went and took a seat.

Kyle contemplated everything as the fields whizzed past. And the further that he travelled from town, the freer he felt, knowing that he was leaving town behind, far, far away. He really needed to speak to his mum.

'Mum?'

'Kyle?'

'Mum, I've just bumped into Daryl again. He's threatened to kill me, I'm on my way back to work.'

'Aw God, Kyle, look, can't you just go to the police now? Enough is enough!'

'No, Mum. If I dob Daryl in, I might end up dobbing whoever is higher up than him in. If I do that, I'm totally dead, someone will find me in the end. Mum, I'm going to send you a picture of him threatening me. Just so you know what he looks like and who he is.' Kyle took a snapshot of Daryl's face on the video. He had thought long and hard about whether it was the right thing to do or not, but he felt that he had little choice.

'Please, Mum, whatever you do, don't tell the police, or I'm dead, totally dead.'

'OK, Kyle, I trust you, but look, are you sure you don't want me to send this to the police?'

'No, no way, Mum. I'm going to try getting his number, I've got something else to send him, all this on a video. He doesn't know where I am at the moment. If anything happens to me, then go to the police.'

'But it'll be too late then, Kyle.'

'Look, Mum, you've got to trust me on this, I know what I'm doing. Look, I got out of trouble last time, didn't I? I need to do it my way. Maybe he'll get fed up and if I'm out of sight I'm out of mind.'

There was a long pause.

'OK, Kyle.'

'Mum, do you trust me? Now? After everything?'

'Yes, Kyle, I do.'

'If he comes round, you don't know where I've gone. Change my phone number to an old number, keep me in your phone under a different name. Anything.'

'OK.'

'And if he does, make sure you get a number for him so I can send him the video.'

'OK.'

'Look, I'll phone you later, I've got to change trains now, OK?'

'OK, Kyle, I'm giving you until the end of the week to sort this out. After that, I'm going to the police. Love you, Kyle.'

'It's a deal. Love you, Mum.'

Kyle got ready to change trains for the one for the coast. He scanned the platform, there was nobody else around. To catch the next train, he would need to go down the road and under the train bridge. Kyle left it a few minutes. He knew that the train station was full of cameras. He was safer here than moving for a minute. He waited twenty minutes and then took his chance. Again, he saw no suspicious cars or people that looked remotely familiar hanging around. But by now, everyone was a threat to Kyle – everyone.

26th June 2020

Kyle hadn't slept all night. He had eventually drifted off to sleep in the early hours of the morning. Then, just as he shut his eyes he sat bolt upright a few minutes later. Every single creak and groan of the old building heightened his fear that it was Daryl, attempting to break in to find him. He could taste the salt on his tongue; the palpitations in his heart ramped up to a crescendo which began to slow down only when he realised that the sound that he could hear was the wind rattling on the windows outside. Every sweat gland, hair follicle and nerve in Kyle's body was on high alert, pumping with the adrenaline that had whizzed around his body for the past two days.

It was no good, staying in bed where he couldn't see anything in the dark was doing his head in. He got up and made himself a cup of coffee. Then he made another one. This would be the only thing that would keep him going today. He could barely face the thought of going to work, but he could not bear the thought of staying here, in this building.

'Move quicker, you've been on it half an hour,' yelled Neil as Kyle scrubbed the floor of the ward.

Neil was the last person in the world that Kyle could bear to be around. His level of agitation was at an all-time high. Every time he heard Neil's annoying voice, he just wanted to punch him.

'No, I haven't been here half an hour, Neil.'

'You haven't done that bay yet…'

'That's because I've been told not to, someone's passed away in there.'

'Well, can't you scrub around them?'

Neil was not only a total tosser, but also a callous one.

'The guy's dead! I've been asked not to go into the bay by the staff on the ward until they sort everything out first!'

Neil stormed off to the nursing station, demanding answers as to why Kyle had been asked not to clean around the bay in question. Kyle shook his head as he listened to Neil reeling off his cleaning policy, which appeared to bear little resemblance to that listed in the induction pack that Michelle had given to him when he had first started his job.

'There's a dead man in there. It needs cleaning when we've taken everything away and he is sealed up waiting for transfer,' said the nurse in charge. Shortly afterwards, Neil came storming back over to him.

'Get scrubbing in there… now!' he ordered, pointing to the bed where the man who had passed away was lying.

'No.'

'You what?'

Kyle had had just about enough of Neil. He squared up to him. Neil was dwarfed by Kyle's six foot frame. He really was pathetic. His flabby face was becoming redder with every step that he took towards Kyle. His comb-over shook under his hair net. Kyle wasn't willing to take any more. Tomorrow, he would ask the agency if he could be moved somewhere nearby to work that was out of Neil's remit. He could tolerate him no longer. Kyle reckoned that there must be other cleaning jobs in and around the hospital that had nothing to do with Neil. Besides, he had enough money saved to pay for accommodation elsewhere for a good few weeks.

'They've told me that they don't want it doing yet…'

'And I'm telling you to mop it!'

'No chance. You mop it! In fact, you can mop the whole floor yourself, you're nothing but a tosser anyway!'

'If you wanna stay in this job, you'd better start toeing the line.'

Kyle put his mop down. 'I don't want to stay in this job, I'm going back to college after my GCSE results.'

'Yeah? Right you are. Think you're gonna pass do you?'

'I've already passed all my mocks, Neil.'

Neil swore under his breath, and walked off, shaking his head.

Kyle could not be doing with Neil today. Plus he still had another two hours of his shift left. Later, Neil, who was in a particularly rotten mood, came storming over to him.

'Why are you still here? I told you to go to the other ward.'

'Yeah, OK, I'm going now, Neil.'

Neil swore under his breath. Kyle heard what he said, it was a crude racist term. Usually Kyle would have become enraged at the slightest hint of someone being racist towards him. But today, he was just too tired. Instead, he decided to play Neil at his own game.

'Calm down, Neil, now stop being racist, you'll give yourself a heart attack, and look how red you've gone, I bet your blood pressures gone right up… breathe now… Stop talking.'

'How dare…' Neil's mask had now begun to slip down his nose.

'Pull your mask up, please, what if there's COVID around here? You're going to be at high risk with your weight…'

'You what? How dare you? Are you callin' me fat?'

'I think that the clinical term is obese, Neil. It's doing you no good, you really should calm down, think of the strain on your heart…'

One of the nurses checking a patient in the bay began to snigger. Hearing this, Neil turned on his heels and stormed back off again.

Kyle needed a job. He couldn't just leave! How would he afford to pay his rent? There was no way he could go back home! Much as he hated working for Neil, he had to. He telephoned the HR department and spoke to the cleaning officer.

'I can't work with Neil anymore. Have you got any other cleaning positions? Somewhere he's not working? I can't stand it any longer.'

To Kyle's surprise, far from being annoyed with him like he thought that they would be, it was almost as if they were expecting his call. The lady on the other end of the phone advised him that they had a cleaning vacancy in the mortuary. Kyle got the distinct impression that this was not the first time that people had had difficulty getting along with Neil.

The mortuary was only just over a mile's walk from the lighthouse, nearly in the town centre. It was a separate entity to the hospital. People weren't keen to clean in the mortuary due to the risk of COVID and the obvious grim risk of encountering dead bodies. It wasn't as many hours, but the pay was better. Kyle wasn't bothered at all by this. He would rather a job – any job – where he didn't have to work with Neil. As he walked back home, Kyle stopped thinking about Daryl for a bit and sniggered to himself as he thought about the look on Neil's face when he realised that he was even more short-staffed than he had been before – now maybe he would actually have to do some work.

30th June 2020

Dangerous as it was, cleaning the mortuary was a much nicer job than working for Neil. The place was cool and airy, and there was nobody around to boss him about. His cleaning was overseen by the mortuary assistant, a man called Grahame who looked as if he was a bit younger than Grandad.

Kyle had been thinking about who else to send the video to. Mo was too risky and could be put in a compromising position. Everyone knew that they were friends. Eddie too. He needed to send it to someone else, someone who wouldn't tell anyone, someone who understood, someone with sense, someone that nobody knew that he was as close to as he was. He looked again at the video. Kyle edited his voice and blanked out Daryl's mouth and the sound every time he said "Kyle". Happy that there was no reference to him on the video, he dialled Roxanne's number.

2nd July 2020

Kyle's mind was running on overtime. He took ages to get to sleep, ruminating over everything. The average of less than three hours sleep a night that he was getting was beginning to take its toll. When he did drift off to sleep, he would wake up a few hours later with a sharp bolt, and palpitations rising in his chest. Sometimes after this, despite the fact that he could not switch his mind off, after a few hours he felt that tired that his body would shut down and he would crash. And then just as dawn was breaking, his alarm would go off for work. Despite the fact that he had seen and heard nothing from Daryl, he had recurrent nightmares about him. He would dream that Daryl had broken into the accommodation and was there, with his gun, or his knife. Kyle would wake up in a pool of sweat. The nightmare would be so real that it would take him some time to orientate himself to the fact that he was alone. He had been feeling jittery, anxious, looking behind him to check that nobody was following him.

It didn't take long for Kyle to begin to miss his mum and his grandad terribly again. He missed his friends. Later that day, his mum phoned him with some bad news.

'Kyle, he's been round here.'

Kyle's heart froze.

'Daryl?'

'Yeah.' His mum sounded shaky.

'Wh…what did he say?'

'He wanted to know where you were. He threatened that if I didn't tell him I'd be very sorry.'

'Shit, sorry, Mum. I can't believe he came to the house.'

'I didn't ask his name, or let him know I knew who he was.'

'Was it definitely him? What did he look like?'

'Er, well, skinny; sharp, weathered face; really mental green eyes that kind of pierce into you, not in a nice way; it was the guy in the photo you sent me.'

'What did you say to him?'

'I played it cool. I said if he was a friend of yours, then please could he ask you to come back home because you wouldn't tell me where you'd gone.'

'What did he say?'

'That I was bullshitting him. Then he grabbed me round the throat and told me to tell you that you're dead meat.'

Kyle's heart sank. A curious mix of shame, anger and guilt rose up in his stomach. Daryl had gone to his mum's, and it was all his, Kyle's, fault.

'I'm sorry, Mum, this is all my fault. Mum, you're going to have to come and work up here, with me.'

'Sorry, Kyle, but I'm going to the police – I told you I'd give you a week.'

'No, Mum, whatever you do, don't do that! Not just because they'll kill me, but because they'll kill you!'

'No, Kyle, what if he finds you anyway? You're going to have to do something; if you don't go to the police about him, I will.'

'No, Mum, please don't do that. I can't go to the police. If there are more of them, they'll kill us both for grassing. We'll be looking over our shoulders for the rest of our lives. Please, Mum, and please tell me you got his number.'

'Of course I did.'

'I've got a plan. It's the only plan I can think of to get him to leave us alone. Please, Mum. Just leave it for a couple of days; I've got a plan.'

The plan involved Roxanne and a burner phone.

3rd July 2020

All Kyle could do was wait. If the plan that he had made with Roxanne didn't materialise, he was dead meat. Either that or he would have to go to the police, and spend the rest of his life on the run.

The mortuary was near maximum capacity. Hospital management had said that it was fuller than it had ever been and that soon they would need to store the bodies in the temporary field hospital mortuary that had been set up in the old leisure centre in town. Cleaning the mortuary was usually a pleasant job compared to the hospital. The area where the post mortems were carried out was built of smooth polished concrete and was easy to clean. After Kyle had finished cleaning the post mortem area, he just had the freezer areas to do and he was finished.

'Evan, I'm off in a minute. When you're finished just switch the lights off mate. No doubt we'll be getting an influx tonight again.' Said Grahame.

'Yeah, sure.'

'I've locked up, just pull the door behind you when you leave.'

'No problem.' Grahame left and Kyle got to work scrubbing area around the freezer.

'Aw, Evan – lovely name, very Welsh - can you just do this bit?'

The voice was not Grahame's. Kyle froze. He turned around slowly.

'D…Daryl. What are you doing here?'

'We need a very serious chat, Kyle.'

'H…how did you know I was here?'

Kyle had not told anyone that he was working in the mortuary. Even his grandad thought that he was still working in the hospital.

'I've got ways and means, Kyle.'

'B…but they, that's confidential.'

'Yeah, it is, isn't it?' Daryl began to laugh. 'Anyway, Kyle, put your mop down, you won't need that where you're going, you're coming with me.'

'No chance.'

How had Daryl found out where he was? This wasn't the plan. The plan was that Roxanne was supposed to use the burner phone that he'd sent her to send Daryl the video that he had taken. Then he'd hopefully leave Kyle alone.

'Aw yes you are, Kyle.' Daryl began to walk towards him, pulling a gun out of his pocket.

'I've got a video that I think you should see, Daryl.'

'Stop right there. Put your hands up. Now move.'

There was nobody around. Grahame had left. It was just Kyle and Daryl.

'No, Daryl, I've got a video I'm going to show you.'

Daryl cocked the gun.

'It's very interesting, I think you need to see it.'

'I've already seen it, Kyle. And you're going to talk now, you're going to tell me who you've sent it to, then I'm gonna shut them up too. You're going to come with me now, Kyle, and I'm going to teach you a little lesson, then you're going to apologise to me, and you're going to do what I tell you to do, Kyle, or I'll take you somewhere that nobody will ever find you.'

This was not supposed to happen. Kyle had felt so sure that once Daryl saw the video, he would leave him alone. He hadn't banked on this.

Kyle's blood ran cold. Images of Jason lying in ITU flashed through his mind. He was in serious trouble. And there was no way out. Kyle looked around the room in desperation. There was only one thing for it. Only one place to go. Pretending to put his hands up, Kyle moved slowly towards the mortuary table. As he neared it, he pushed the concrete slab on top of it off with all his might towards Daryl. It flew into his legs, causing him to topple backwards. The gun went off, firing a shot at the ceiling. As it did so, Kyle made good his escape.

'Bastard.' Daryl screamed in agony.

Kyle ran down the side of the building, still half-dressed in his protective equipment. He scaled the fence adjacent to the hawthorn hedge at the front of the mortuary, managing to reach up onto the wooden top, oblivious to the prickly thorns, some of which managed to become embedded in his leg as he ran down the path at the side of the mortuary which led to the costal path.

As he ran, Kyle tore the remnants of his protective equipment off. It was no good, he had to buy some time and phone the police – he would have to. This was crunch time – he would have to deal with any repercussions after. His mum and grandad had been right – he should have just phoned the police all along and taken the consequences.

The weather was on the turn. It had gone from blazing sunshine this morning to a blustery gale in less than a few hours. The tide was on its way in and the sea was choppy.

There was only one thing for it. Kyle continued towards the lighthouse and reached the start of the path, looking back over his shoulder – sure enough there was Daryl, less than a hundred metres behind him, running with a slight limp, looking angry, very angry. Then he shook his fist at him and retreated. Kyle's adrenaline dropped slightly; maybe he had decided to leave it for now? Maybe. But one thing was for sure, Kyle had to get out of the area as soon as possible. Kyle hoped that he wouldn't try to follow him. There were still enough people around to ensure that Daryl would find it difficult to do anything without drawing attention to himself, but further up the path with the impending gale would be a very different story. There was only one place that he could hide that could buy him some time until the police arrived. He dropped his sprint to a jog and continued up the path.

But as Kyle got approximately halfway to the lighthouse and the harbour, he heard a faint sound behind him – the sound of an engine. There was a tarmacked track next to him, but this was reserved for emergency vehicles only. Surely Daryl hadn't managed to open the barrier? Kyle turned back around. In the distance, he could see a cloud of dust, with Daryl's car advancing at great speed towards him. There were around 200 metres of the road left. Adrenaline flooded through Kyle's body as he sprinted down the remainder of the path. All the time, he could hear Daryl's car coming closer and closer. There was fifty metres left to go. With all his energy, Kyle ran as fast as he could towards the shore. As he reached the end of the path, he heard Daryl's car screech to a stop with seconds to spare.

He couldn't take the path around the bay - by the time he got to the middle, he would be exposed with no cover should Daryl decide to shoot at him. The few dog walkers, cyclists and people mooching about on the path were becoming fewer and fewer. He continued at speed up the path and away from Daryl.

Kyle looked out to the sea. The tide was coming in, the rocks just about visible to the naked eye. Despite the fact that he could jump the rocks with his eyes shut, the sea was becoming perilous. At around the half way mark, the rocks, now covered in seaweed, became more slippery and uneven than usual. Kyle hesitated, was this a really bad idea? As he approached the shore where the rocks started, Kyle looked around. After about a minute, the people milling around would all disappear around the corners of the bay. Kyle looked further up the path; there was nobody there for the next half a mile or so. Kyle realised that he could use the impending bad weather to his advantage.

If he could just get across to the lighthouse, he could use his phone to call the police once he got to the island, maybe keep Daryl talking across the bay while they came. Maybe someone had already noticed that he had driven illegally up the path and they would come anyway? All he could do was pray.

Gasping for breath, Kyle proceeded into the sea and ran across the rocks. He had to get across before the last person disappeared out of sight, before Daryl could draw attention to himself by firing his gun again. As the waves ripped over the rocks, covering and uncovering them, Kyle darted across. As he got half way across to the part where the rocks became more perilous, he nearly lost his footing and fell into the sea. In the now foul weather, he could hear Daryl's voice bellowing from behind him. Kyle still had another twenty metres of the rocks to clamber across. He noticed the last people walking about to disappear around the corner. Praying that they would not look back and see him, Kyle slowed down and concentrated hard on jumping over the remaining rocks.

'Kyle, come back here.'

Kyle turned around, pretending to look extremely shocked that Daryl was there. In desperation, he continued hopping over the rocks. To the naked eye, to someone who had no knowledge of the rocks, he simply looked as if he was running through the shallows towards the harbour and the lighthouse. As he reached his destination he looked back. There was nobody except Daryl in sight – he had pulled out his gun. Kyle reached the rocks of the lighthouse and took cover around the side.

'Kyle, I mean it, I'll fire. You can't hide there forever, Kyle, I'm coming to get you. I'll kill you, Kyle.'

Kyle emerged from behind the side of the lighthouse, leaving the majority of his body covered.

'You'll have to, Daryl. You're gonna have to kill me before I'll come back.'

Hesitantly, Daryl pointed the gun at Kyle.

'Go on then, Daryl, you're gonna have to do it, you're gonna have to shoot…'

'Don't make me do it, Kyle! I'll …'

'Yeah, go on then, you're gonna have to, Daryl.'

Kyle pulled his phone out ready to phone the police as Daryl stepped onto the first rock.

'Great choice of place, Kyle. I'm gonna kill you and chuck you straight in the sea – there's no one around now, you'll never be found, Kyle.'

Daryl was making his way towards him, across the increasingly treacherous rocks. Only a fool who did not know their way would do that – but Daryl, full of bravado was proceeding. Kyle paused and put his phone back into his pocket. It was becoming clear that Daryl was not familiar with the rocks – he would undoubtedly have caught up to Kyle by now if he had been.

'Go on then.'

'Don't say I didn't warn you, Kyle.'

Daryl had managed to get half way across and was just about to jump onto the more perilous rock. He fired a shot. Kyle ducked behind the lighthouse. The bullet missed him completely, hitting the other side of the concrete harbour. Cautiously, Kyle popped his head out at the side. Daryl was now hesitating at the place on the rocks where Kyle had faltered – so near, but yet so far. It was becoming apparent that he was in trouble.

'Is that the best you can do, Daryl? Are you sponsored by Specsavers?'

'You shut up!' Daryl shouted, his hand visibly shaking as he gripped the gun.

Furious, Daryl stepped out onto the slippery, uneven rock. From there in, the path was tricky. Once again, he fired the gun. This time, the bullet flew straight into the ocean. It was becoming increasingly clear that Daryl had no idea about how to aim a gun properly.

'Aw, you nearly got me there, Daryl. What you aiming for? Belfast harbour?'

'You… you shut up.'

'You'll have to come and get me, Daryl!'

'Na, I'm… I'm… just gonna follow you onto that rock and kill you then. There's no one around, Kyle. You'll be washed out to sea without a trace.'

'I wouldn't come through here if I were you,' said Kyle. 'If you do, you'd better hope your sense of direction is better than your aim.'

'Oh yeah? You think I'm scared of a bit of water?' replied Daryl as he attempted to manoeuvre across the fifth rock in. As Kyle looked back, Daryl was already in trouble. The waves were coming faster now. He struggled over the next rock and, as Kyle watched, he faltered and fell into the mud below. Unbeknown to Daryl, this tip of the estuary was no sandy beach and the current below at this level of water was deadly. Daryl had no hope of escape unless he quickly got back onto the rock. He seemed to panic, and thrashed about instead of keeping calm and trying to climb back up. He was soon submerged up to his waist, and instead of using his hands to try and wedge himself free and jump back onto the rock, he clung onto his gun and tried to point it at Kyle. Kyle remained partially hidden behind the lighthouse just in case Daryl fired the gun by accident and had a lucky shot. The rough waves began to crash into Daryl, quicker and faster. Only thirty metres or so away from Kyle, Daryl was out of his depth and sinking fast. In desperation, he pulled his phone out of his pocket, but the next large wave that came washed over it. Freeing his hand to try and cling onto the rock he dropped it into the sea.

'H… h… help,' he cried.

Kyle scanned the bay. The beach and costal path were deserted. The day trippers and walkers had disappeared along with the fine weather. It was just him and Daryl now, together with the sea and a gale force wind coming in.

'Kyle… h… h… help me!'

'What?' said Kyle, poking his head cautiously from behind the lighthouse, 'like you helped Jade? And Jason? Like you planned to do away with them? Like you did to the last Bic that you had no use for?'

'I… I… I dunno what you're talking about,' Daryl gasped as he floundered around. 'Just help me, come back and get me.'

'Yeah you do, Daryl. The ones you took to Hereford?'

'Kyle? Just… please… help me, get a rope.'

Kyle shook his head.

'What for, Daryl? So you can shoot me? Are you scared, Daryl? Are you as scared as the Bics that you threw into the quarry in the back of the car were? Or as scared as Jason and Jade were when you kidnapped them?'

'I…I'm sorry, Kyle. Just help me.'

'Then turn around, and go home, Daryl, I ain't never working for you again.'

'Kyle, help me. I can't! I… I don't want to kill you really, Kyle, I promise!'

'Yeah, you've just tried to shoot me, Daryl, remember?'

'P…p…please, Kyle, I'm sinkin'! I'm gonna die! You can't just leave me here… help me!'

'What, so you can kill me?'

'N… no!'

As a huge wave ran over his body, Daryl dropped his gun into the sea. There was no doubt about it, Daryl was now firmly stuck, floundering around in the waves that were coming right up to his neck. This would be easy. All Kyle had to do was let the water come in, until it covered Daryl's head and his airway and stay out of sight. Maybe at some point, someone would come past, see Daryl and call the coastguard. But by then, it would be too late.

But this wasn't Kyle; this wasn't Kyle's nature. As he watched Daryl, he began to feel uncomfortable. Even though Daryl had just tried to kill him, it felt odd, strange, unnerving, watching someone about to die, in a situation that he, Kyle, had kind of created. He would have to live with that for the rest of his life.

'Kyle, Kyle!'

'OK, OK, I'm gonna ring the coastguard now, Daryl. But they're going to ask questions, Daryl, questions about what you're doing there, and who you are, especially when the camera footage is shown of you firing a gun at me. I've got footage of you doing things that you shouldn't do, Daryl.'

Daryl's face was white.

'If I go missing, sooner or later, they're gonna put two and two together, it'll be murder, Daryl. You think you're invincible? People know about you, Daryl. My family know about you, so do my friends! If they connect me to you, Daryl, they're gonna ask questions. How can I explain that I'm in the same place as you when you get rescued? The rest of the gang aren't gonna be happy with either of us, they'll kill us both, Daryl.'

'I… I'm sorry Kyle. Please, help me. I promise… I never wanted to kill you. Come on, help me, just help me!' said Daryl, in between trying to avoid swallowing gulps of seawater from the incoming waves.

The easiest thing to do would be to just leave Daryl there, but then that would make Kyle a murderer. With every second that passed, Daryl was in more serious trouble. Maybe Kyle could get the last person that he saw walking up the costal path towards the harbour to phone the police, if he hopped over the next set of rocks to the ship and ran after them that's what he could do.

Why, oh why couldn't he just leave Daryl in the sea? After living on his nerves, after having to leave his friends and family, after starting to have hopes and dreams, everything was shattered. After everything, Daryl had won. Kyle felt certain that if he was rescued, Daryl being Daryl would soon forget about Kyle saving his life and hound him until he could make him re-join the gang. It was no good, by phoning the police, Kyle's number would be traced to Daryl being in the sea. Kyle would surely be given protection but then have to go deeper undercover. How he would miss his mum, his grandad, his friends. His heart sank as he contemplated it all. Reluctantly, Kyle pulled his phone out of his pocket and unlocked it.

'Don't worry, Daryl, I'm phoning the coast guard. Help's coming soon.'

'Kyle!' Daryl continued to flounder around in the mud. The water was now further up his body as the incoming waves nearly submerged him. 'Don't leave me!

But as he went to dial the number, his phone went blank. Damn, he hadn't charged his phone for the last couple of days! Now what?

It was no good, treacherous as the conditions were, Kyle would have to hop across the rocks to the harbour and find Cliff; maybe Cliff could help him take a boat out?

Then, something happened.

A figure appeared on the costal path from behind the ship. Kyle's glasses were dripping with water, but he could just about make out a person on the shore.

'Help,' cried Kyle, waving his arms across the bay to the person on the shore. 'He's drowning.'

Appearing to notice Daryl in the water, the figure on the other side of the bay walked up to the edge of the sea.

'Please, I need your help, there's a man in the sea, drowning. Please can you call the coastguard.'

It looked like a lady. Kyle was unsure if she had heard him in the wind and rain.

H… h… help me,' said Daryl as he used his arms to battle the waves.

'Please, help him, phone the coast guard!'

Kyle watched as she pulled a phone out of her pocket and appeared to make a phone call. Unable to hear, Kyle watched as Daryl desperately splashed around in the sea.

Kyle's whole life played out before him. He had nearly used his own phone to phone the police. Had this happened, they would have asked him questions. Now, the lady on the opposite shore had seen him, what if she had sent the helicopter for him too? How would she know that Kyle was OK and could climb over the rocks onto Cliff's harbour when the storm settled? If they tried to rescue him too, now the police would be asking him, Kyle, questions and all this would have been for nothing.

Even though the rain and wind seemed to be calming down, Daryl had sunk lower into the mud and the waves were by now crashing over his head. If help didn't arrive in the next few minutes, Daryl would surely die. If he died, maybe his body would never be found, it would just drift off in the water, out to sea; maybe it would be washed up on a beach somewhere. There was nothing more that Kyle could do. He began to wonder if he should just risk clambering over the big rocks to the side to the harbour where Cliff was to see if he could do anything. With the sea calmer, he felt sure that he could make it. Then who would ever know that he had witnessed the whole episode? His conscience was clear, he had tried his best and his intentions were genuine.

Then something very odd happened. The lady on the other side appeared to finish her call and throw her phone into the sea.

As the weather calmed, Kyle thought that he could hear his name being shouted in the distance. Maybe it was Cliff? Maybe he had come out to see what the commotion was about? Kyle looked over to the harbour, but Cliff was nowhere to be seen. He looked over to the shore.

'Kyle, Kyle.'

Kyle would know that voice anywhere, that wasn't a random lady standing on the shore - that was Roxanne!

'Rox, Rox!'

'Kyle, are you OK?'

Even though the rain had slowed down, and the wind was calming, Kyle could only just about hear what Roxanne was saying. He felt that to shout back was futile. Kyle raised his thumbs up to Roxanne.

'Do you need help?'

Petrified that she might phone the coastguard for him, Kyle shook his head vigorously and moved his arms across his chest in a cutting direction.

'No!'

Rox nodded and put her thumbs up to Kyle.

Then another thought struck Kyle; he felt sure that more than one emergency service would arrive shortly at the scene.

'Just get out of here before the cops arrive,' he shouted.

'What?'

'The police will be coming, there's nothing more you can do. Get out of here.'

'But…I can't just leave you…'

'I'm fine, just get out of here.'

Roxanne stood at the edge of the shore for a few moments.

'Please, just go.'

Roxanne hurried off back down the path.

By now, Daryl was getting tired. He had stopped floundering as much. Even though the sea had calmed and the waves were no longer crashing over him, if help didn't arrive soon, Daryl would be dead. Kyle watched him for a few minutes, contemplating what to do. There was only one thing for it, he would have to hop over to the harbour and get a rope. Now that the conditions were less treacherous, Kyle knew that he could make it.

Then, somewhere in the distance Kyle heard a whir of helicopter blades making their way through the sky, a little dot in the distance, coming closer and closer. Kyle ducked down underneath an upturned boat next to the lighthouse. He peeped through a gap at the side and watched as the helicopter neared; it hovered closer, moving downwards towards the water where Daryl was. A rescuer in a harness was lowered on a ladder with a rope and buoyancy aids, reaching out to grab Daryl's arms. Kyle's heart began to beat faster as he watched. As the rescuer grabbed him, the grip on Daryl's arm loosened. No longer splashing around, Daryl was now mostly submerged under water. The helicopter continued to hover right over where Daryl was and the rescuer once again grabbed Daryl's arm. Eventually, placing what looked like a rope and rescue aids around him, Daryl's now limp and shattered body was winched out of the water and up into the helicopter.

Kyle watched as the helicopter swiftly flew off in the direction of the hospital.

Then the police arrived. They stood for a few moments, looking around the beach. With nothing or nobody to see, they left shortly after. Kyle felt sure that they would be more interested in seizing and investigating Daryl's car that he had left up the track than staring at an empty beach.

The sea was calming down. As the police disappeared around the side of the old ship to where Daryl had left his car, Kyle decided that it was safe to jump over the remaining rocks to Cliff's harbour and around the shore to make his way the long way back down the costal path, being extra vigilant and taking care to avoid any police that may be patrolling the area.

****

Soaked, shattered, and in a state of disbelief, Kyle arrived back at the accommodation and plugged his phone into the charger. He sat down on the bed and put his head in his hands. What had just happened? As his phone started up, he dialled Roxanne's number.

'Rox, what just happened?'

'A long story, involving me arriving at the mortuary as he did and hiding in the back of his car. It was easy to get into, it's a shit car.'

'Jeez, Rox, you could have been killed! What if he'd have found you? Or crashed? And your phone? He'll trace you…'

'Na, I used the burner you told me to get to phone the police. Anyway, are you kidding? I've never had so much fun in my life. It's the most exciting thing that's ever happened to me, especially in the last five months.'

'Rox, I owe you my life.'

'You do.'

'Where are you anyway?'

'In a café in town waiting to hear off you. I was gonna give it an hour and take a walk back to see if you were still stuck on the rock by the lighthouse.'

'Rox, give me fifteen minutes to get a shower. I'll meet you by the big clock in the middle of town.'

'Anyway, when I meet you, will you take me back to your grandad's mate's lighthouse?"

'It's the least I can do.'

5th July 2020

Kyle had given in his notice at the mortuary and asked for a transfer back to Michelle's team. Not that he had been in work - he was technically off sick. After the episode with Daryl, he had had to return to the mortuary later that afternoon and replace the concrete slab back on the table before anyone noticed. After much heaving and straining, he had managed to put it back, but he had felt his back go into a spasm as he had used all his might to push it back into place on the top. As incapacitated as he was, that did not stop him from clearing his room, packing his bags and making his way back home on the train.

Before he had left he had managed to find out that Daryl had been transferred to ITU. He was now stable and had a constant police guard.

Later that day, just as he arrived home he had a call from Grandad.

'Kyle, I need a fry up from Shone's.'

A fry up from Shone's. Kyle had craved a fry up from Shone's every day for the last few months. They were now doing takeaways, or you could sit outside at the front or in the back.

'Well, I'll come with you, Grandad, but you can't sit inside, it's too dangerous, we'll have to go outside.'

'I don't give a stuff anymore, I'm sick of all this virus business, it's all going away anyway.'

'No, Grandad, crammed public places are where everyone's getting it from. I'll come with you, but we're sitting outside. Come on, it's a nice day.'

'Well, I'm blooming sick of all this.'

'Look, Grandad, I know, but it's still kicking around, still circulating. Everyone thinks it's gone, but it hasn't. You're not totally safe, not somewhere like Shone's. Anyone who's been in there could have it.'

Grandad huffed on the other end of the phone.

'OK, outside then.'

'Meet me in twenty minutes.'

Kyle walked through town to Shone's café. How amazing it was just to be able to walk down a street in town, not having to look over his shoulder.

Grandad had not yet arrived; there was only one table left outside. Kyle ordered himself a coffee from the waiter. He sat down, relaxing in the bright sunshine with his thoughts. Even though the tables had been moved as per social distancing guidelines, his table was still within earshot of the two men sitting next to him. As he sat waiting for Grandad, Kyle could not help but overhear their conversation.

'So how does it feel to be out?'

'Alright. It was shite in there to be fair, the worst time I've ever done. Because there was corona everywhere, we had to stay in the cells and not go near each other.'

'So how did you get any gear in and out?'

'It was hard, mate, really hard with the restrictions. Had to utilise some of the dodgy screws.'

Kyle pulled his phone out and pretended to look at it, not wanting to make it obvious that he was listening in on their conversation.

'Anyway, we can get the gear going again soon, since the restrictions are easing up we can start not looking obvious again.'

'Yeah, mate. Although they're on my back. If I get caught again, I can't do another stretch in there like that, nearly drove me mad.'

'I know. It's all nearly over now though? Nearly back to normal. Once the kids get back out and about, it'll be easier to recruit some new Bics.'

'Yeah, they'll be desperate for the money.'

'One line's already gone down, the Hereford one, cops caught up with Daryl Santos, looks like he's tried to do away with himself, drown himself in the sea. He's been arrested.'

'Well, plus he ain't exactly been inconspicuous has he? Half killed one of the Bics a couple of months ago, three of them missing with talk of him pushing cars into quarries? He's looking at a long stretch.'

'Yeah, and Bert found out the gang were tryin' to do away with him, knew too much, so he's apparently been talking, got nothing to lose, has he?'

Grandad appeared.

'Alright, lad? You ordered yet?'

'No, I was waiting for you.'

'What they doing here? I'll go in and order.'

'Sit down, Grandad, they're coming out to us. You don't want to go in there, specially without your mask.'

'Bloody mask, they won't get me wearing no bloody mask in a cafe, pal, I'm sick to death of this bloody thing. People telling me I can't go out, then you can go out, nobody knows their left from their right! Then it's safe, then it's not.'

'Yeah, alright, Grandad. Do you want your usual?'

'Yes, fry up and a coffee. I'm bloody starvin'.'

Shortly after, their breakfasts arrived.

'This is bloody good stuff,' said Grandad as he smothered his bacon with brown sauce.

'It is. I've missed coming here.'

It was just like the old days, the days before the virus, when Kyle and Grandad were free and could go and do whatever they liked. Well, almost; Grandad seemed a bit quiet. This was most unlike him. Almost guarded, as if something was bothering him. Not anything to do with anxiety or the virus. When they went to Shone's, they usually had their fry up, a couple of coffees and put the world to rights. But not today.

'Do you want another cup of coffee?' asked Kyle after Grandad had finished his fry up.

'Er, no, mate.'

'What's up with you today, Grandad?'

'Nothing, son.'

'Go on.'

'Well, to be honest, I don't think I like sitting outside. Can we go somewhere else?'

'Are you jokin'? I thought you loved it here. You haven't been for months, have you?'

Just then, Kyle noticed the men on the table next to them getting up to leave. He caught the eye of one of them. He stared hard at Grandad. Then he stared at Kyle. He looked intimidating, hard, angry. Kyle decided that it was best to avoid eye contact. But Grandad didn't seem scared.

'So, Kyle, what you going to do today?' asked Grandad, staring at the man.

'Dunno. Roxanne said she's going to teach me and Mo to play the guitar, she's been practicing with her band. I've been looking at getting a second hand electric one.'

'Well, see if you like it first, mate,' said Grandad. He still seemed preoccupied and it was something to do with the man at the next table.

The man staring at grandad had been the man who had been complaining about being in prison. His brow was furrowed, his eyes narrowed, narrower than Kyle's. He had deep creases around his eyes, deeper than they should be, as if he had had an unhappy life. His pin-pricked pupils suggested substance misuse. He looked sallow, and agitated. Kyle had seen that demeanour before – it was the demeanour of loss of self, like people that he knew who had lost hope in life years ago. But why was he staring at Grandad like he was when he didn't even know him? Then the other man spoke.

'Chad, mate, you've left your phone on the table.'

Chad!

Kyle's heart raced faster, his throat dried up in shock. Was it him?

As the men left, neither Kyle or his grandad spoke. Eventually, Grandad broke the silence.

'Well, on second thoughts, maybe I will have another coffee.'

'That was him, wasn't it, Grandad?'

'Who, son?' asked Grandad, unconvincingly.

'My dad, that was him!'

Grandad stared hard at Kyle.

'How do you know?'

'Chad, he said his name was Chad. And he looks and sounds like he's not a very nice person.'

Grandad shook his head slowly.

Kyle looked away for a few seconds. How could that be his dad? That person? He looked and sounded like a scumbag! No better than Daryl! And he was talking about recruiting kids and dealing drugs! How could *he* be in any way related to Kyle? He was nothing like his mum. What could she have seen in him? Surely it was all a mistake?

'Him?'

Grandad nodded slowly.

'Him?' asked Kyle again, in disbelief.

'Yes, Kyle.'

'B…but I don't want him to be my dad.'

Grandad didn't speak for a few moments.

'Why do you think your mum has never encouraged you to meet him?'

'But he's just like Daryl. I heard him tell his mate he's just got out of prison. That can't be my dad, I don't want to be like that.'

'I know you don't, son. And you're not. But that's because of how your mum has brought you up. How she's kept you out of trouble, worked hard so you knew that was what normal people did, taught you respect and manners. She's the reason you're not like that.'

Kyle had waited for so long to find out who his real dad was. Where he had come from, what he looked like. And now he knew. Knowing was worse than not knowing. Now that he knew, Kyle wished that he had not found out. He never wanted to be associated with, or have anything to do with someone like that ever again.

In his darkest days, he had thought that maybe his family had it all wrong. That his dad was a bloke who was alright. That there had been some misunderstanding between him and his mum, lack of communication maybe? That he was a good bloke, like Grandad was; someone who would take him to football, keep him on the straight and narrow, see him at weekends. But, no, there hadn't been, had there? The childhood dreams that he harboured of him had just smashed to smithereens somewhere in the centre of Kyle's head.

Kyle wanted his mum. He wanted to go home, and hold her, and thank her for everything. For never leaving him, or giving up on him, for pushing him to do well. The itch that he had felt his whole life regarding finding out who his father was had been well and truly scratched. Kyle would never ask his mum about his dad ever again.

'Anyway, Grandad. I've got someone better than any dad, I've got you.'

20th August 2020

Kyle sat by his phone, anxiously tapping his fingers on his desk. His phone pinged, he picked it up to read the text; it was Mo.

'Crappin' it.'

'Me too.'

Kyle put his phone down. Another ping. Surely this was it? No, it was Roxanne.

'Torture this waiting.'

'Yeah, slow.'

A minute later, Kyle got another ping. With a link to a message. He logged on. There they were! Dare he open them? What would they say? With trepidation, he clicked the button. He had passed them all! An A star in his French, three As and the rest Bs! Yes! They had had faith in him! They knew he was trying, they knew that he could do it!

'Mum, Mum!' he screamed down the stairs.

His mum came running up the stairs. She had taken the whole day off work so that she could be with him when the announcement came through.

'Well?'

'Look, look, Mum,' he said, holding the message on his phone up for her to see. Tears ran down his face. Then his mum started crying too.

'I did it! I passed them all!'

His mum threw her arms around him. 'I knew it, I knew you'd do it, my clever boy, now you can reach for the stars.'

'Thanks, Mum, thanks for believing in me, you and Grandad, when nobody else did.'

She held his face in her hands and started deeply into his eyes. Kyle beamed up at her.

'Oh, I've got something for you.'

'What?' he asked. She handed him a box.

He opened it. It was a new pair of trainers, the ones that he had said that he liked last year, the ones he'd asked her to buy him. She'd remembered. Kyle smiled up at her.

'You said I could have them if I passed all my exams. How did you know I would?'

'I've still got the receipt.' She laughed.

Kyle's phone pinged.

'Smashed them all!'

'Passed! I actually passed most of them!'

'A-levels here I come.'

It was Mo, Roxanne and Cornelia. They had all done it! They had all done it because they had helped each other. This was brilliant, absolutely brilliant: it was teamwork at its best. And if nothing else came out of studying, randomly, from just getting his head down he had met Roxanne. Completely unlike any of his other friends, she was awesome. He owed her his life.

There was someone else Kyle couldn't wait to phone.

'Hi, Grandad.'

'Hi, son, how did you get on?'

'Well, a bit crap really...'

'What? You're joking me…'

'Yeah, I only got all As and Bs…'

Grandad gasped on the other end of the phone. 'Well done, lad, well done! I knew you'd do it. But what next? What are you going to do? You can't waste that brain.'

Kyle shook his head.

'Na, I won't. Planning to look at A'levels, thinking of working with Mum part-time in the hospital.'

'Hey, lad, you don't want to be exerting yourself, doing too much, like.'

'Na, Grandad, I learned a whole year's worth of stuff in just under four months last time. And getting up early? It kinda kept me out of trouble. I can do it - I know I can.'

'Well, OK, son, making an honest living from working hard is much better than doing what you were doing before.'

'No chance I'd do that again.'

'I'm proud of you, son. You're gonna do alright, you know?'

'Thanks, I love you, Grandad.'

'I love you too, son. Well done. Anyway, after you get back with your friends, I'm taking us out.'

'Amazing, Grandad! I'll pop by in a bit.'

'You see? You did it. Because you worked hard. I knew you would. Now have a lovely time camping.'

Kyle turned to his mum. 'And I love you too, Mum. Thanks for everything. Anyway, you made a pact with me - you're coming to college too.'

'I did make a deal with you, didn't I?' she said with a sigh. 'And you know if I promise you something, I stick to it. Looks like I'd better go to talk to Michelle about going part-time for a bit then.'

****

'This is amazing! Don't tell anyone, but I've never been on a train before, I always get the bus.'

As he sat on the train next to Mo, looking out at the open countryside on this glorious day, Kyle's peace was disturbed when something hit him on the side of the head.

He looked at the empty plastic squash bottle rolling around on the floor.

'What a shot,' said Cornelia, sitting next to Roxanne on the opposite side a few rows down.

'Sorry, lost my grip,' said Roxanne, sniggering.

Kyle got up to go to the toilet. As he passed Roxanne, he blew some air into his empty crisp packet, held the end and clapped his hand onto it with all his might at the back of Roxanne's head.

'Aaargh!'

Kyle could hear laughter behind him as he proceeded to the toilet.

'Will you lot stop messing around?' said a lady behind them.

'Sorry,' said Cornelia. 'Come on guys, stop it now.'

'Aw balls to them, it's only GCSE results day once a year, people should lighten up and stop being so miserable,' said Roxanne.

Kyle sniggered to himself. Eddie, sitting at the back with some of their other friends stuck his leg out as he walked past and Kyle nearly tripped over. Guffawing could be heard from the carriage. Today was a day for fun. It was all about a promise that he had made to Roxanne. Best let off the steam before they got there, as Cliff was doing him a favour letting them camp in his field next to the harbour, and had promised to let Kyle show Roxanne the lighthouse. Kyle knew that he needed to be respectful.

But Kyle reminded himself that he was free. So far, he, Kyle, had been in no way implicated in Daryl's capture or demise. It was by now common knowledge that Daryl was looking at a long stretch in jail. The mystery of how Jade's house caught fire remained unsolved and Kyle owed Daryl and any remaining gang members nothing.

Soon, they would be camping in Cliff's field next to the harbour and the lighthouse, Kyle couldn't wait to get back to the place that had saved his life and share all its beauty with his friends.

The Lockdown Series

By Rachel K Parsonage

This is the third book in 'The Lockdown Series', a fictional series about NHS staff working through the lockdown. Other titles in this series include:

The Healthcare Assistant: Escape to Lockdown

The Porter: Retribution in Lockdown

The Cleaner: Evasion in Lockdown

Thanks for reading the third book in 'The Lockdown Series', I really hope that you enjoyed it. Reviews and feedback, positive or negative, are always welcome.

I can be found on Facebook at 'Rachel K Parsonage', author.

Or my amazon authorpage can be found here:

https://www.amazon.co.uk/Rachel-K-Parsonage/e/B08J3F27M8/ref=dp_byline_cont_pop_ebooks_1

Printed in Great Britain
by Amazon

69465153R00119